DEAD MAN'S TREASURE

Also by Max Brand

DEAD MAN'S TREASURE

MAX BRAND

A NOVEL OF ADVENTURE

DODD, MEAD & COMPANY
NEW YORK

ISBN: 0-396-06879-0
Library of Congress Catalog Card Number: 73-15034
Printed in the United States of America
by Vail-Ballou Press, Inc., Binghamton, N.Y.

CHAPTER 1

The chest was long, deep, and wide, covered and water-proofed with number one sailcloth, varnished. It was as heavy as a water-logged boat, and when Perique laid hands on the twisted rope at either end and lifted, the weight of the burden surprised him and made him sink to one knee. He could hear the groan and thunder of the surf on the reef near the mouth of the harbor as he relaxed. It sounded like a rising storm.

Off to the right, a party of the Lanua natives were spearing fish by torchlight, stepping over the rocks with the raised torches dripping gold and the spears lifted for the stroke.

On most of the South Sea islands he would have paid no attention to the big Polynesians, but this was the first time he had landed on Lanua, and his reputation might not have traveled before him.

The gleam of the blowing light stained the heaving water around him as the hunters came closer, and now he picked up the chest as though it were a wicker laundry-basket and carried it lightly up the rocks. They made the going bad. Some of them were sleeked over with ocean moss as slippery as oil; others showed their teeth to him; but Perique had eyes in his feet and swiftly came to the beach.

Even there he would not step on the sand because the Islanders read footprints as white men read books. Instead, he chose the heads of some wave-worn stones that projected above the beach, and on these he moved till he had reached the brush.

Through the brush he went as a snake goes, sensing the way until the stars were shut out above his head by the

1

foliage of enormous trees. The ground became dry underfoot; he could smell the bark.

He needed a tool to open that box, since he lacked the key to it; so he returned to the beach. There, from the verge of the brush, he watched the golden bodies of the natives. One of them made a strike in a big fish that knocked the water to a spray before it was flung back onto the beach.

The Lanuans laughed, holding up their hands. But Jim Perry, whom the world called Perique, did *not* laugh. His mouth watered. His eyes grew dim. He was starved enough to have eaten that entire fish.

When the party went on, he plucked a fifty-pound stone out of the sand. A lighter one might have done as well, but when you make a choice, it's better luck to stick by the first bargain.

Perique went back through the brush carrying that boulder in one hand, lightly; and with an instinct as true as that of a homing bird he came straight to the sea-chest. There he tossed down the rock and sat down to feel the chest all over with his hands.

The darkness frightens most of us. The fear of the unknown lunges toward us, takes on a gigantic semblance, whispers together in conspiring numbers; but Perique, lost in the darkness, trusted his ears and the nervous brain of his fingertips. So he saw that box from end to end, located the lock, and numbered the bolt-heads around it. Afterward he picked up the rock and smashed the good steel with three powerful strokes.

Before he so much as lifted the cover of the treasure, he sat on his bare heels to listen, his eyes closed, his head tipped to the side. The only sound was the trade wind, rushing like a mountain stream through the branches high above him. He waited through a long moment, to make sure that no living thing was coming in the direction of the noise he had just made.

Then he opened the chest.

2

The voyage ashore had not upset the seamanly order in which everything was arranged in the chest. His diving, twisting fingers found the roughened hilt of a knife in a shagreen scabbard, the hard, cool surface of some white ducks, the chalked leather of some white shoes, thin silk shirts, light linen ones, the solid butt of a .45 caliber revolver, a number of papers, some books, more shoes, an oilskin wrapped around a package, a sewing kit, some rolls of bandages, medicinal tape, a case of small bottles, two folded hats, neckties of rough silk, four-in-hand and bow, handkerchiefs, spare shoelaces, playing cards, pipes laid side by side in leather cases, a jointed fishing rod, some old newspapers, a magazine or two, and finally what he wanted most of all—matches.

He did not strike one at once. There were only three in the box, and there was no use wasting any of them for half a glimpse at the contents of the box. He went first to the trees, where he found some strips of dead bark to tear away with fingers like the talons of a bird. There was green brush also, and when he came to a faintly aromatic smell, he knew that the foliage was rich in inflammable oils. So of that particular bush he took armfuls which he laid down close to the stem of the nearest tree. The trunk would act as a screen to half the light of his fire, at least.

The head of the first match sparkled on the side of the matchbox, then went out; the second one ignited and presently some of the leaves were flaming. Others he twisted hard into small torches that could be lighted one by one; too great a flare of fire was not what he wanted. It was true that Lanuans were not apt to venture far into the dark of the forest by night, but there was a millionth chance that some prowler might be around, and Perique was a fellow who counted the millionth chance.

The flickering of the light showed him in the center of a grove of huge banyans, or a tree of that family. The vast jagged trunks spurted out branches that cascaded down toward the ground but merged into other trunks before they reached it. The effect was that of a vast crypt under a cathedral, with pointed vaults such as the thirteenth-century builders used.

Perique observed the scene deliberately, holding up one of his torches, from which the light spilled over his body. He was naked, without even a loincloth, but the darkness of his skin lessened the nakedness. He would have been no more offensive, to the most modest eyes, than some old Greek bronze. Besides, he was built like an Islander.

Perique was like the Islanders except for one essential difference. Your South Sea vegetable eater is soft, but Perique was not.

His nickname, in fact, was not an idle chance but had a meaning. In the States, down in Louisiana, where they grow the strongest mules and black men in the world, they also grow the strongest tobacco; but even that strength is not enough for those who want volatile pepper added to the smoking mixture. So some of the tobacco of a chosen sort is woven into vast ropes which then are twisted. Under the shed those long ropes ripen; every day a twist or two is given. The rope diminishes. It becomes at last a straight cord no bigger than your thumb, black as the devil, and strong as fire with the concentrated juices of the leaves.

A few pinches of it will flavor a pound of chopped tobacco; it is the garlic of the smoker's world; and its name is *perique*. That was what they called Jim Parry because the soft flow of his lines was deceptive. The muscles of a mule look smoother than those of a horse, for instance. And, besides, there was enough spirit of a certain sort in Perique to season an army of men.

When he had observed the forest about him for a moment, he picked up the chest, carried it close to the tree, and pulled open the lid again. In this manner the light was effectively screened on two sides. On the other two it slid away

4

through the woods, but that was a chance he would have to take.

He took out all the clothes. The eyes in the tips of his fingers already had seen the contents thoroughly enough, and about all that the light could tell him was a matter of colors. When the chest was empty, he began to tap the sides and bottom, not with his knuckles but with the hard, rapid tip of a forefinger, twisting his head over to listen. It was in the lid itself that he heard a slight, a very slight, hollowness. He examined the canvas, ripped a portion away, and found beneath it a little teak panel which pushed back at once.

Inside he found a bit of piled silk which unwrapped from a fold of paper, and on the paper in black ink with red labelings of names was a small chart. He studied that chart for a moment, then tilted back his head and laughed noiselessly. After this he examined the clothes, tried them on. The owner of the chest had been a big man. His trousers were a little too large for Perique around the hips, and the coat pinched him more than a little across the shoulders; but he could belt in the trousers and the coat would remind him to stand straight.

A white linen shirt was much too small for his neck, but it was better style anyway to go with the shirt open at the throat. The shoes were large enough for his feet; the socks fitted as though made for him; and the white duck hat would stay on his head.

The revolver he put away dexterously in his clothes after he had made sure that there was not a single mark of personal identification on it. The knife was branded with initials. He hesitated about it, then shrugged his shoulders. He took the knife by the point between thumb and forefinger, picked out as a target a branch fifty feet above his head, and whipped the knife into it. For a moment the shiver of the blade sent down a humming sound like that of an angered wasp. A slight shudder ran through the body of

Perique, but, after all, he was something of a fatalist; and it seemed fairer to God if not to man to leave some clue for eyes keen enough to find it.

A moment later a stinging doubt made him go to the tree and lay hand on the rough of the bark, ready to climb; but again he shrugged his shoulders and turned his back. He would give the thing no more thought, after this, for Perique was not a man to hesitate more than once.

The clothes and the gun and a little purse of gold coins were all that he took, except for the paper. This he fitted under the insole of his right shoe, and then carried the stone and the chest, with all its contents, through the forest until he had put several of those vast natural bays between himself and the banyan tree in which the knife remained, dimly glimmering.

Here he broke the chest up small with the stone, corded up the fragments, and set them on fire. Afterward he sat down with his back to a tree trunk and watched the thick smoke rise and tangle and spread among the upper branches like the growing ghost of a tree. When the fire had burned out, he gathered the iron fragments and carried them back to the beach.

To throw them into the sea was his first impulse. Instead he picked out a stone so huge that even all his power hardly could make it lean aside. Under it he dropped the metal bits and let the boulder rock back into place, puffing out a living breath of air. Then he went toward the lights of the town.

CHAPTER 2

The town of Tupia used to be limited to its hill alone. That was in the old days before the English secured a "protectorate" over the Lanua Islands which, according to their

6

ancient formula, they eventually turned into a "possession," Lanua becoming a portion of the British Empire in the strange, drifting way that gets to results without marked or sudden steps. With the English came the English peace, quietly based upon an occasional British gunboat and its rifled guns.

A high-power shell exploding in a jungle is such a manifest act of God that the native mind cannot resist it. This sort of logic created by degrees the bloodless or almost bloodless revolution which turned the Lanuans into peaceful British subjects and put the copra business and the control of the pearl fishery into British hands.

With the extension of the English peace, when the town dwellers came to understand that the more savage inland tribes no longer would be apt to rush at them in the night, the Islanders began to leave the crest of Tupia Hill and build their thatched huts nearer and nearer to the shore of Tupia Bay.

The thing was not done in a moment. A year or two after the first villagers ventured on building their huts outside the walls of the town, some of the inlanders actually delivered a night attack and cleaned up a lot of random loot plus a good number of heads.

The English have written rules for their game of empire building, and among those rules is strict protection for the subject peoples.

Therefore it was not at all strange—though the Lanuans never expected it—that a British battleship put into Tupia Bay and landed a column of marines who marched slowly into the interior of the island, dragging certain small guns with them.

There was little or no fighting. But before the expedition there had been half a dozen flourishing hill towns, and after the expedition there were none. The auxiliary column of men from Tupia loaded itself with the possessions of the inlanders and then the towns went up in smoke.

Of course the villages were rebuilt afterward, but everyone on Lanua had learned a salutary lesson: that it may be fun to make an attack at dawn or twilight and spear the enemy as he rises out of sluggish sleep, but if one does such things, the British come with rifles that shoot with magic accuracy and burn both the house and the household goods.

Among other loot the expedition came back from the hill town carrying with it several hundred packages wrapped securely in palm leaves. The English had hoped to bring back the score of heads of the Tupia villagers who had been speared in the night. To make sure they had done a good job, they took every sacred head they could find and opened a great trench in the beach of Tupia and buried the leaf-wrapped lot.

Afterward they blew taps, fired three volleys over the grave, and went back on board their warship. They had had a pleasant little excursion and they had dulled most of the Lanuan spears forever. It was true that in the hinterland some savage people remained who were apt to make unguarded travel perilous, but on the whole Lanua had been inducted into the English peace. And afterward the villagers of Tupia no longer needed to climb the tall hill at the end of their day's fishing. They could go, instead, at once into the big huts which they constructed near the beach.

That was why the hilltop gradually turned into the white man's town, where the traders lived. Of course most of the population up there remained native, but these were the Islanders who were employed in the storehouses or in the shops, or as domestic servants or entertainers, or, above all, in the wide domain of Bill Smith's Tavern.

Bill Smith was an English ex-prize-fighter who, for a number of good reasons, did not dare to return to his native island. But he had put up an establishment at Tupia so full of mixed opportunities for European and Lanuan entertainment that the fame of it had traveled all through the South Seas.

That was why Perique, with English gold in his Yankee pockets, headed straight up the hill of Tupia. He was hungered to the starving point, but he would not eat until he could get the best that money could buy.

He hardly had reached the slope of the hill, above the beach, when he heard a great sound of wailing. A throng of the natives were running toward the largest hut in sight, and the splashes of firelight rippled like living gold over their bodies. Inside the hut a woman began to scream. Her voice came out of the doorway, now, like a red torch through the quiet of the night. She saw the white clothes that announced the presence of a white man, and she ran to the big American with both her hands flung out. She turned into a tall, slim girl. By the flash of her teeth and the gleam of her eyes, so to speak, Perique saw Konia for the first time. He forgot the hunger of the belly for the moment, and ran with her into her father's house.

It was a big interior with great tree trunks used instead of beams to uphold the roof. There was a sweet smell of island cookery in the air. Yonder on a nest of palm leaves lay a big roasted fish, half devoured, and in the middle of the floor lay a fifteen-year-old boy twisting his limbs into knots, gasping, with protruding tongue and outthrusting eyes; his face was not golden brown but purple.

On the mat beside him, on his knees, was as big an Islander as Perique had seen for many a day. The father was holding up his huge, vain hands and half-shouting, half-groaning a prayer.

Perique stood over the lad and looked down at him for a moment calmly. There were a hundred natives, at least, ringed around the circumference of the room; and they uttered a brief, tingling cry of protest when they saw the indifference of the white man. When he had made up his mind, he leaned, caught the strangling boy by the ankles, and heaved him up shoulder-high. When his dangling head was a foot from the floor, Perique dropped him with a shocking jar.

The father saw this dimly through the mist of his agony. His action afterward was a swift reflex. He leaped to the next pillar, caught a knife with a blade a foot long out of a shark-skin sheath, and ran at the throat of Perique. But then he saw that the lad had not broken his neck. Instead, he was sitting up gasping a red froth from his lips and drawing great hoarse breaths.

Instead of knifing the American, the big man dropped to his knees beside his son and began to babble questions. It was Konia who picked up the crooked fishbone from the ground and held it up for all to see, and a shout of delight welcomed the sight of it.

Most of the men went out at once, now that the affair was ended so tamely, but the women followed more slowly. They had begun to laugh, their black eyes twinkling with admiration of the white man.

"Thank him, Kohala," they said to the big fellow. "He has saved your Liho. Thank him, Konia, for your brother's life."

Still they were laughing as they went out. And Perique would have followed them, except that the girl had one of his hands and was pressing the back of it to her forehead, and big Kohala had another which he was using in the same way.

The girl was saying that the American was her grand-father; Kohala was declaring that the stranger was his father; and young Liho, getting to his feet, began to rub his sore throat and stare at the deliverer. The lad already was as big as most mature Europeans. Their language was perfectly familiar to Perique.

"I'm glad that you found me, Konia, and let me come to help."

He got them up off their knees in this manner just as a voice said, near the door, ". . . Perique!"

Perique jumped for the doorway like a bird off a bough, stooping at a field mouse. He came back into the dim flicker of the firelight holding the wrists of an old man. Kohala grabbed the fellow from the other side angrily.

"What have you done, Maku?" asked Kohala.

The old fellow looked up at Perique and smiled. The smile was a twisting grimace on his broad, battered face. He looked like a gray-headed Irishman with a touch of grim old Irish humor. The darkness of his hide was an anomaly.

"Shall I speak the word again?" asked Maku. "Shall I call you Perique?"

Well, there he had used it again, and Perique glanced swiftly toward the others in the house. His name had traveled very far through the islands, but it was known in various ways. He heard Kohala whisper at once, "Taboo!"

But that did not mean everything. It meant a man set apart from others, either because he was nearer to the gods or to the sea-devils. The look of frightened concern with which Kohala accompanied the word had a greater significance than the word itself. The children took the name harder still. Liho dropped to the ground and covered his face with a strip of grass matting; Konia flung up her hands. But instead of blinding herself, she kept peering between her fingers at the white man.

This was all pretty bad. It made Perique wish that he were on board a ship sailing as fast from Lanua as the wind could blow it or steam-drive it. But since there was trouble in the air, it was as well to face it boldly.

"Now, what do you know about me, father?" he asked. "Tell me, Maku. A man who knows only half the way often loses himself in the forest."

"I am a man," said Maku modestly, "who has traveled a great deal. Wherever the wind blows or a paddle can move the water, Maku has gone. Therefore I have heard more than others. I know many things too big for the hearts of foolish men. I have heard what the wind tells the sea. But I am not a child. I do not speak everything. What the young moon saw on Apia beach—four angry men—let the moon.

speak of that."

A cold finger, as it were, ran curving down the shoulder and side of Perique. He was remembering that night clearly enough, and that same young moon, a sickle of gold in the western sky. For that matter, he never would forget it. Besides, one does not forget moments which have been underlined by knife strokes. They had come in at him, all three, from three sides, with the bright steel glittering in their fingers. He had had only his bare hands, in the beginning, but afterward . . .

Big Kohala, hanging his head, would not look at the savior of his son. The terror of the girl, however, meant more to Perique than all the rest, somehow.

He took a breath and then said, "My friends, I shall not be very long in Lanua. If you make a bad taboo of me, people are going to be sorry that I came to your island, and they will make me very sorry, too. So I ask you to say nothing about that other name. My real name is Jim Parry. And for your silence I will pay you . . . the fishbone which Konia still is holding."

He laughed a little when he said that. The others did not laugh. The silence stretched out as long as a snake. Then Konia uncovered a jar and poured some white milk into the rind of a coconut.

"Shall we all drink from this bowl and so become friends?" she asked.

Kohala, recovering from his dream, exclaimed, "Yes! We must do that. I feel the cold taboo in the blood nearest my heart."

"Will you drink with us, Maku?" asked the girl.

The old man stared at Perique and grinned, or seemed to grin, but that might have been merely a contortion of his face that came with the squinting of his narrowed eyes. He muttered something that no one could hear, but the girl took the answer for granted.

"Good! That shows you are a friend of this house, Maku,"

12

she said. "Liho, get up!"

His muffled voice answered from beneath the matting: "Konia, I am afraid . . . I am afraid of the taboo!"

She kicked him with her bare toes. "Get up, Liho, or I'll call you a coward."

This threat made Liho rise slowly to his feet, pale with fear. He could not look higher than the white shoes of Perique.

Konia spilled a bit of the milk from the rind and sang very softly an old Lanuan song.

The last part of the song Kohala accompanied with a rumbling bass; Liho joined with a trembling voice; Perique sang also, looking curiously at old Maku. But the veteran was silent. They had all ended.

Konia cried out in a breathless whisper: "Maku!"

The old man started. Then he lifted his hand slowly toward Perique and said deliberately: "Oh, my friend!"

"Good! Good!" cried the girl.

And they drank from the bowl, in turn, the milk of the coconut.

CHAPTER 3

Bill Smith used to say that when a man got as far south as the South Seas, and yet not quite in hell, he ought to have everything he wanted, so long as he could pay for it. Therefore Bill Smith set up his tavern on the hill of Tupia and put together everything that a man could wish for.

When Perique got to the top of the hill, he found a lofty palisade built double and filled in with earth so that it made a real rampart, and around that rampart went armed men of the sort you can find in the South Seas. "Dirty white," they might be called. They all are apt to look Irish red or Portuguese black.

13

The red-faced ones look like whisky bloat and the dark fellows have the wine-sour look about the mouth and eyes.

It is hard to say why men should fall into these two distinct classes, when they are the "dirty whites" of the southern islands, but so they happened to be. Perhaps the in-betweens die young. Those fellows perambulating the wall—there were three of them—caused Perique to look up and scan the nearest of their faces.

And then he smiled just a little. He recognized the type perfectly. The repeating rifles they carried and the revolvers on the hip were not there for nothing. Every one of those guards was a picked man and knew how to shoot straight—and often.

In the center of the front wall of Bill's tavern there was an arched gateway, and inside the gate sat a huge man who filled a device that was half chair and half hammock. His face descended in three folds of which the first was the forehead, the second was the cheeks, and the third was a great pendulosity under the chin. His central body section expanded in a vast billow. On his head he wore, though it was night, a shining white sun-helmet. His white shirt was open down to the hair of his chest. He had on white duck trousers and was, in fact, all white man to the feet. These were shoved into native sandals, of woven grass, the coolest and the lightest things in the world. The fat toes of Bill Smith showed. They were as rosy as though they had been rouged.

"Good evening, Smith," said Perique.

"Good evening," said Bill Smith. "Don't I recollect you in the Government House at Melbourne, sir?"

"Perhaps you do," said Perique, "coming in or going out. What have you got here that's worthwhile?"

"Anything that a man could wish," said Bill Smith, "from Bass's ale, so cold that it'll make your teeth ache, to roast pig and a comfortable bed—with trimmings."

"What has trimmings?" asked Perique. "The pig or the bed?"

"Both, sir," said Bill Smith, and grinned.

He was one who made up his mind quickly, and now he felt that he knew his man.

"Get about an eight or ten or twelve-pound pig roasted for me," said Perique. "I'll have some Irish whisky with it, and some siphon. And with the pig, to ease it down, some of that seaweed salad, a couple of sections of roasted breadfruits, a few bananas, and some Mawmee apples. I'll have a spot of raw fish to commence with—some of the little fellows that go down head first—"

"And that wriggle on the way?" asked Smith.

"That's right," agreed Perique. "And you can leave in a few slices of roasted yam. Have you any Egyptian cigarettes?"

"I've got some for my friends," said Bill Smith.

"We knew one another at once," said Perique. "Now I want a place where I can see the stars and the sea while I eat and listen to some music. I want something to look at, too."

Bill Smith stood up. "If I could remember your name, sir," he said.

"Parry," said Perique.

"I'm going to make you right at home, Mr. Parry," said Bill Smith.

The seaward side of the tavern dipped down from the height of the hill a little, and there, on an upper terrace, the eye traveled over the top of the parapet and went far out across the Bay of Tupia, and across through the starlight and the moonlight to the hills on the farther side of the water. The moon's path gilded the water, and where its golden little torrent was not flowing, the stars freckled the waters softly, here and there.

Perique sat on the veranda of a little four-room native-built hut, with windows cut into the sides; one of those windows opened right in the face of the parapet, and therefore it was secured with strong steel bars. Out in front, on the veranda, a table was spread for Perique.

Two Islanders came hurrying and sweating to bring him

his food in courses. A little fountain gushed up nearby, and in it the whisky and the siphon were kept cold. On the table the white bones of a ten-pound roast pig were showing as Perique carved deeper. He ate hugely, without haste. And his starved body began to feel ease creeping over it, an ease sweeter than sleep. He drank until he felt a certain numbness of the palate. He could hear his own breathing.

"But where's the music?" asked Perique. "And where's something to look at?"

Bill Smith, absenting himself from his other business, had been watching this meal with a consuming interest. Bill himself ate several times a day, but when even he saw a "real man" eat a real meal, a certain mixture of envy and brotherly affection stirred his heart.

It was stirred now almost more deeply than it had ever been. And he said in his native tongue to one of the Islanders, "Bring the three best; you know them. Two to dance and one to sing. Island songs, Mr. Parry?"

"Island songs," said Perique.

So, presently, a guitar began to thrum, and two girls started the undulations of the Lanuan dance. It was a semi-religious affair, that dance, but it was in worship of some of the powers of nature, and it was such a thing as would hardly be seen in a church. Perique looked at the pair with lazy eyes.

"Send them away," he said to Bill Smith.

"Send them away?" echoed Bill. "Wait a minute, sir. Moonlight's not good enough for the two of them. They ought to have an electric spot. This couple would knock London dizzy. There ain't any knees made straighter than what the pair of them have. If you went and ordered a pair straight from the shop, you wouldn't find them any better."

"Send them away," said Perique.

Bill Smith started an angry answer, but permitted it to end in a wordless snort.

"What have *you* seen on Lanua?" he asked, after he had

16

waved the dancers away.

Instead of answering directly, Perique merely said, "Tell the girl with the guitar to get out of my sight, somewhere near, and sing that song about the salt of the sea. D'you know it?"

He tilted back his head and sang in a soft voice with a hum of resonant power behind it that famous Lanuan song which goes:

> I have come in from the sea,
> The salt of it has cracked my lips,
> The salt of it burns in my eyes;
> My belly is sick with the taste of the sea,
> But now I tread the shoaling water,
> The soft sand is under my feet,
> The green of the forest blesses my eyes,
> And the wind laughs in my heart and over my head.

He had not sung three verses when the guitar player, now hidden around the corner of the wall, began to join in the lines. Her voice went up on high wings, soaring lightly above the deeper tones of Perique.

When the song ended, Bill Smith said, "I see. You been here before. You got it under the skin."

"I've got it under the skin," admitted Perique.

Bill Smith was called away, and a moment later his voice was booming out its deep bass notes on another veranda close by.

Perique could hear him saying, "Good evening, Mr. Coffee. Glad to know you, Mr. Ellis. I seen you before, but never up here. Sorry to hear about the *Nancy Lee* sinking, Mr. Coffee."

"Never mind the *Nancy Lee*," said the answering voice. "I think about the poor devils who went down with her, and I thank God that Ellis managed to take his life out of the sea."

"A close call, eh?" asked Bill Smith.

"The closest you ever saw," said the third voice. "It was the Thumakau Reef that got us just as we were sliding through the gap. I'd left the ship in charge of my first mate, Harry Lee. The ship was named after his daughter, you know.

"And I'd hardly gone below when something went wrong. I'll never know what. I heard the crash.

"When I got on deck again, we were going down by the head. In five minutes we were under water. I got hold of a plank. Tore up my shirt and lashed myself to it. And ten hours later a big Fijian thamakau came bowling along, with the sheetman keeping the outrigger clear of the waves, just kissing the top of 'em. I thanked God when I saw that boat, and managed to hail her. That's how I managed to get back here. There was a chief called Kamakau on board the boat, and he went out of his way to drop me outside the harbor. That's why I'm here."

The captain of the lost *Nancy Lee* was still finishing this speech when Perique walked from his veranda onto the veranda of the adjoining little house where Matthew Coffee, the trader, sat beside a brown-faced young man.

That was Ellis, the late master of the *Nancy Lee,* big as a barn and crammed full of powerful manhood.

Perique said, "How old are you, Ellis? I thought that I'd find you up here, but not this soon. . . . You're Matthew Coffee, aren't you? My name's James Parry. . . . I think you owe me a drink, because I was the fellow who spotted your captain from the thamakau when we were zipping along like a flying fish."

Ellis, as this speech began, had started up from his chair with a black face. But as it ended, he was waving a hand.

"Sit down, Mr. Parry," he said. "Shake hands with Matthew Coffee, and sit down. . . . Find us some of that old special whisky, will you, Bill?"

18

Bill Smith went swaying and puffing away, as Perique leaned a hand on the edge of the table and smiled down at the two men. He paid little attention to big Ellis. Most of his regard was for Matthew, a middle-aged man with a sallow skin and hair as greasy black as that of any Islander. He had a steady, brilliant eye.

As soon as Bill Smith was out of the way, Ellis said, "Now what in hell do you mean, Parry, or whoever you are, or want to be?"

He was half rising as he spoke.

Matthew Coffee said, "Sit down, Ellis. . . . You mean to say that you don't recognize Mr. Parry? Wasn't he on the boat that picked you up, after all?"

"Of course he wasn't," said Ellis.

"The *Nancy Lee* was wrecked on Thumakau Reef, was she?" asked Perique. He kept on smiling down at them.

"What's the matter with the man?" asked Coffee.

"Thumakau Reef," said Ellis. "That's what I said before."

"And the outrigger came along and picked you up, eh?" asked Perique.

Ellis was silent, staring. And the more he stared, the more his two eyes shrank small and bright in his head.

"What do you get out of this, anyway?" he asked. "What are you after?"

"Why, I just dropped down on Lanua out of the sky," said Perique.

"But that way of reaching an island doesn't sound so good, does it? So I thought it might be better to arrive with Ellis, here, on the same boat with my old friend and cutthroat, the Chief Kamakau. . . . You remember me now, don't you, Ellis? It doesn't matter. While the chill was still in you, you let Bill Smith think that you recognized me well enough.

"You'll do as a letter of identification for me, Ellis."

"You know," said Ellis through his teeth, "I've got a damned good mind . . ."

19

"I don't understand all this," said Matthew Coffee.

"The hell you don't," said Perique, and laughed in his face.

At that moment the special whisky arrived, and an instant later Perique was saying above the brim of his glass, "I drink this standing. . . . To you, Coffee. . . . To you, Ellis. . . . And to every man that ever was saved from sharks, in the sea or on the land."

CHAPTER 4

The governor of Lanua was the Honorable Irvine Glastonbury. He came from an old family which had showed few weaknesses to the world, but the Honorable Irvine was the rift in the lute. He had risen in the political world for a time by undertaking certain pieces of scavenger work such as have to be performed even in the most reputable of countries and by the most high-minded of political parties. We are all human, and politicians are the most human of all. Irvine Glastonbury had become so early mature that he was soon ripe, soon rotten, as the old proverb has it.

However, his associates were all honorable men themselves, and they had not the least intention of letting him down. When his name and fame became a stench in London, his fellows in the Conservative party chewed their thumbs for a time, but at last they decided to bury the Honorable Irvine in the South Seas.

Better men than Glastonbury had been put on the skids and have arrived at places even farther away from Piccadilly. The Honorable Irvine made a few scenes, discovered that this was all he could get out of the pocket of his party, and therefore he went down to Lanua to represent the state and console himself with gin and other devices.

He was one of those tall, pale, bloodless Englishmen, and

behind his big glasses he looked like a Bible student, or even a missionary, except for one unfortunate feature. Like a red flag in time of peace, his nose flamed huge and swollen in the middle of his face and made mouth and chin and eyes and forehead all seem dwarfed by the contrast. The Honorable Irvine was not unaware that his nose was an affliction, and he had developed a habit, when assuming an attitude of thought, of covering his proboscis with his hand.

He was covering his nose in exactly that manner this morning as he sat in his office, keeping his regular office hours. Those hours began at the earliest possible moment. The Honorable Irvine was wakened every morning at the crisp hour of eight, at which moment a servant entered the governor's bedroom with a short drink of gin, with a squirt of siphon in it, and a squeeze of lemon.

The Honorable Irvine said that this drink cut the sleep out of a man's eyes.

When he was able to sit up, it was about eight-thirty. He then went to his bath, which was a pool thirty feet long, incised in the living rock. There he swam leisurely for a time, climbed out, submitted to a thorough rubdown, and had, in place of breakfast, a longer drink of Holland gin with a smaller squirt of siphon and a larger squeeze of lemon in it.

By this time he had arrived at clothes for the morning. By the time he had got himself into them and had been driven down to the governor's offices, it was about ten.

Two hours of endeavor had brought the Honorable Irvine to his place of labor, where he examined the papers which were laid before him by his secretary, Hulbert Wilson. This Hulbert Wilson was one of those astonishing coves who can work ten or twelve hours a day even in the tropics. He sweated his soul out to keep the governor from making a holy show of himself and getting into serious trouble with the Foreign Office.

He knew that the governor despised him, and yet he continued to labor earnestly in behalf of the Honorable Irvine.

England and America are full of people like that, devoted to the machine, trying to roll the wheels uphill, no matter how the jackass at the point of command tries to steer the mechanism into the gutter.

With the assistance of Hulbert Wilson, the Honorable Irvine used to get through an assortment of papers, and sometimes his strength would last until as late as eleven-fifteen, but at about that moment he neared collapse. The tropical heat began to get him down, and he realized with sickening suddenness that lunch was not far away, and that his appetite required some strenuous bracing before he could attempt to look food in the eye. So he always left the office with a rush, snapping commands over his shoulder as he went.

On this morning Hulbert Wilson was explaining a certain legal problem that had come up. The governor had just burst into an impatient exclamation and sprung up from his chair, crying, "Great Gad, Wilson! Eleven-fifteen and lunch hardly more than around the corner. I've got to get out of here. . . ."

Here Nancy Lee, a young lady, was announced. The governor heard her name, took a quick, deep breath, and looked at himself in the mirror at the side of the room.

He said, "Damn it, Wilson, the girl is going to be a wreck. Father just was killed, wasn't he?"

"Yes," said Wilson.

"Fell off a cliff or something when he was drunk, Wilson?"

"No. He went down on the *Nancy Lee* at Thumakau Reef."

"How did Matthew Coffee happen to name a ship after the daughter of a man who was only a first mate?" asked the governor.

"Coffee thought it would be a popular move, sir. And the house of Coffee and Coffee needs popularity."

"Why, Wilson? Always seemed to me that Coffee and Coffee was a firm founded on bedrock."

"In fact, Matthew Coffee is as hard as rock," said the secretary.

"Well, let the girl in," said the Honorable Irvine. "But why the devil should she choose this early time in the day?"

Nancy Lee came in, not dressed in mourning. She was all in white. She had on thin white gloves, and she carried a white parasol with a green lining. The thin brim of her hat cast a film of shadow over her face. But her smile seemed as bright as ever. She went up to the governor and shook hands.

She said, "I have something to tell you that ought properly to go to the judge. But since he's away on leave, you're both the legal and the executive power, aren't you?"

"I'm whatever you want me to be," said the governor firmly. "You tell me what's the matter, Miss Lee, and I'll put it right for you with my own hands."

Nancy Lee looked down at the rather shaky hands of the governor, and then she looked back at the red bulb of his nose. A moment later it was covered by the thoughtful hand of the Honorable Irvine, for the girl was saying, "I don't think that the *Nancy Lee* came to the end that everyone says. I don't think that she sank on Thumakau Reef."

The governor said, "Well, well, well, well, well! My dear Nancy Lee! Not sunk on the Thumakau Reef? Well, well, well, well, well . . ."

"On the street this morning," said Nancy Lee, "I saw a man wearing one of my father's white duck coats."

"The devil you did!" said the Honorable Irvine. "What a lark—I mean, what a devilish shock that must have been! . . . Where did he say he found it?"

"I didn't ask him," said the girl.

"Why not?" asked the governor.

"I thought it would be better for armed men to make the inquiry," said Nancy Lee.

"Ah, you mean you think he might be a trouble-maker?"

The girl said, "He's a big, powerful, soft-voiced man. He has a pair of eyes that take hold of things—and move them!"

"What's his name?"

"James Parry."

"Why, that's the fellow who arrived with Ellis on the outrigger," suggested the governor.

"If he picked Ellis out of the sea," said the girl, "did the captain of the *Nancy Lee* have my father's duck coat along with him? Do you think he was wearing the coat to keep himself warm in the sea?"

The governor thought, and then shrugged his shoulders. "That doesn't seem likely," he admitted.

"No, it doesn't," said the girl.

"But the point seems to be," said the Honorable Irvine— "the point seems to be . . . ah, what *does* the point seem to be?"

"This: How did James Parry get my father's coat?"

"But he never was on the *Nancy Lee,* was he?"

"So he says."

"Ah, is that the point, then? You think that he was on the *Nancy Lee,* and perhaps got the coat from your father, and . . . but Ellis says that Parry was *not* on the *Nancy Lee,* but was on the outrigger that picked Ellis out of the blasted ocean, and all that. You've heard that, haven't you?"

"I've heard it," said the girl.

"Wait," said the governor. "Wait a minute . . . White duck coat . . . there are millions of white duck coats in the world, Miss Lee. You know that?"

"There aren't millions that have a little jagged tear just above the wrist on their right sleeve, though," said the girl. "Not many that have that tear and that I've mended."

"Ah . . . ah . . . ah," said the Honorable Irvine. "You think . . ."

"I think that the *Nancy Lee* may still be afloat somewhere. And I hope and pray . . . that my father may still be with her . . .

"But whether he's living or dead," she went on, "I want to find out how this James Parry came by my father's coat! I

24

want the officers of the law to take a hand with him. . . ."

"By Gad, Nancy Lee," said the Honorable Irvine, "I'm going to do just that. The police! Of course! I'll send the police for him, of course. I'll get half a dozen of them after him this moment!"

CHAPTER 5

Perique lounged in a hammock on the veranda of his private cottage at Bill Smith's Tavern. A big shadow, wallowing over the grass like a hopping toad, came rolling up to the hammock.

It was Bill Smith, dripping with perspiration which rolled down over the triple folds of his face. He said:

"How's the morning with you, sir?"

"I'm satisfied," said Perique. "How did you sleep?"

"Bad," said Bill Smith. "Damn bad, sir. I got to thinking and wondering. Maybe I was getting old. Maybe I'd lost the knack. I advertise a place up here where a man can come and be at home. And then I don't give them what they need."

"What more do I need, Bill?" asked Perique, blowing a thin blue stream of fragrant smoke into the air above his head.

"You need," said Bill Smith, with a large grin and yet with an air of pathos also—"you need what every boy that's been raised proper ought to have. You need a woman's influence around the house. What's equal to the touch of a woman, Mr. Parry?"

"Nothing," said Perique.

"I mean," elaborated Bill Smith, "what is there to keep a man home away from the troubles and the dangers and the money-spending of night life, as you might say."

"Bill," said Perique, "you ought to be a preacher."

"Yes, sir," said Bill Smith. "I've thought of taking up that line, one day; but I'm kind of far away from churches, down here. But as I was saying about women, what's home without a sort of a wife? Where's the welcome, I mean?"

"Exactly," said Perique. "Where's the welcome, as you say?"

"And last night," said Bill Smith, "I showed you the best layout in the way of temporary wives that I could offer, and not one of them pleased you. But this morning I hope it'll be different."

"Bill," said Perique, yawning, "I can see why you're in this business. It's because you have such a great big hospitable heart. Isn't that the reason? It's wanting to make everybody happy that keeps you in the tavern, isn't it?"

"That's what it is," said Bill Smith, with his vast grin which threw up waves of fat across his eyes and almost blinded him.

"Well," said Perique, "you make me happy—and keep women away from me, will you?"

"Wait a minute," said Bill Smith. "Hey . . . wait a minute . . . The minute I seen you, I knew you were a man that was raised with prayers alongside his ham and eggs in the morning, and prayers alongside his brandy and soda at night before he goes to bed. I knew you were a real Christian, Mr. Parry . . . but maybe I have to explain to you that things down here are not like London or New York."

"Well, you can go ahead and explain," said Perique.

"What I mean to say is that down here in the South Seas . . . on Lanua, anyway . . . the native gals don't fence themselves in between a prayer book and a golden ring, the way they do up north. They are liberals, is what the Lanuan girls are. And it makes them kind of sad when they think of a poor white man that comes sailing across the sea and don't find anybody at home when he reaches the place where he's going to live for a while in Lanua.

"It makes them mighty sad, sir. So they say to themselves

that it's better to be a white man's wife once in a while than it is to be married forever to any one of the biggest chiefs on the island. There's more interest to them. Maybe they got a liking for babies with a paler complexion. I don't know what it is.

"But you give one of these girls a string of beads and a kind smile and she'll come up here and keep the house tidy for you, and darn your socks, and all that."

"Speaking of women," said Perique, "I'd like to know the name of a girl who carries a white parasol with a green lining."

"A white girl or a mulatto?" asked Bill Smith.

"White. Very white. Green eyes. Sea green. Brown hair with some gold dust shaken into it. A girl about five feet six and an eighth inches, about a hundred and thirty-one and a half pounds."

"Ah," said Bill Smith. "That's what went and bit you, is it? But you won't get any good out of that. That's Nancy Lee."

"Steady," said Perique. "Nancy Lee is the name of a ship. A ship that sank . . . Archibald Ellis commanding . . . Matthew Coffee owner. Only the brave and lucky skipper managed to save his life from the hungry sea."

"D'you think there's a fake behind that yarn?" asked Bill Smith.

"How could I be doubting anything I hear in a place like Lanua?" asked Perique. "But Nancy Lee?"

"Her father was the first mate . . . Harry Lee . . ."

"That's right, of course."

"Ever see him? Big and broad. A fighting kind of a man and mighty honest. Would have made a fortune except that he couldn't keep away from the cards. But he made himself a good father to Nancy and . . ."

"And so he's left her all alone?"

"I'll just say one thing to you about her," said Bill Smith. "Nancy is the spirit of uplift and Christian progress here in

27

Tupia. She does good works. She goes out and picks the thorns out of the feet of the poor, and pours in iodine. Yes, sir, she's a great worker and healer with iodine and castor oil, in the name of the Lord; and she keeps the faith advancing."

"I see," said Perique. "She is just one of those things, eh?"

"She's just one of those things," agreed Bill Smith. "And now, coming back to the question of a temporary wife . . ."

"I don't want to come back to it," said Perique.

"Last night," went on Bill, raising his voice to overwhelm any interruption, "the selection that I offered you was all right, but not for a man with his eye filed right down to a sharp point, like yours is, Mr. Parry. . . . The trouble was that we didn't have the best to give you. I ain't been able to get the best until this morning."

"What's the best?" asked Perique.

"Why," said Bill Smith, "I been watching her grow up. I been watching her get a couple of years past the usual age for marrying. But still she just let the time go by her, as though it didn't matter. . . . A girl, Mr. Parry, straight as a joint of bamboo and sweet as coconut milk . . . eyes like a starry night with all the damn smoke blowed out of them . . . color like the shady side of a peach, kind of yaller velvet . . . walks like a cat on a holiday; talks like a damn singing bird or I'll eat my hat . . . and when that gal tips back her head and laughs, all the waves come rolling in from the sea and blow their foam in your face."

"Bill," said Perique, "it's no use. I appreciate what you say, though. You've talked enough to make yourself sweat. . . ."

"Talk be damned!" said Bill Smith. "I've *walked* for you this morning, Mr. Parry. I've walked all the way down the hill to her father's house and told her that up on the hill in my place there was the most man that ever come ashore in Tupia Bay. And after I talked a minute, I was able to bring her up the hill along with me."

"Bill," said Perique, "it's no use. I'm sorry. But it's no use at all."

There was no sound except the deep breathing of Bill. Then he said, "You wouldn't even look at her?"

"All right," said Perique. "Looking isn't a promise."

Bill Smith clapped his fat hands together three times, and around the corner into the ken of Perique walked Konia, the daughter of Kohala.

Perique lifted his head.

"Well?" said Bill Smith.

"Bill, go away," said Perique.

"And leave her?" asked Bill.

"Don't be a damn fool," said Perique.

"Sure I won't," answered Bill, and rolled himself rapidly away, making deep chuckling sounds of thunder in the middle of his being.

"Konia, what are you doing up here in this bad place?" asked Perique.

"I have come to my lord," said Konia.

"Your lord doesn't want you," said Perique. "Wait a moment. I'll say that in a different way. You are prettier, Konia, than the green throat of a parrot and pleasanter than the evening breeze. . . . And now you must go home because I'm a very busy man. Wait a moment. Here's some money. Use part of it to buy yourself a few white dresses . . . no, make them blue. Thin stuff that won't make you hot but will keep the eyes of men from handling so much of you."

"My lord, may I speak?" said Konia.

"I would rather hear you talk, Konia, than listen to any other person sing."

"My lord, it is time for you to run from Tupia. Within a little while they will be here for you."

"Who will be here, Konia?"

"The men of the law. They surely are coming with guns for you."

"Why should they be coming for me?" asked Perique.

"My brother, Liho, heard that it was to happen. He ran home to us just before the fat man came asking for me. So I came up the hill to you to tell you. They are coming to kill you, Perique, because you murdered the man on the ship . . . the man whose white coat you are wearing now."

CHAPTER 6

Perique had closed his eyes, as he listened to this warning.

"Did I kill him, then?" he asked. "Harry Lee . . . did I kill him?"

"My lord has the coat of the man," said Konia. "My lord murdered him. Therefore my father and my brother are waiting at the edge of the forest. They will show you the way to a safe place. They will take care of my lord."

"Sing a song for me, Konia, will you?" asked Perique.

"My lord, they now must be very close. They must be nearing this place. Will you rise, my lord, and go with me?

"My lord," she added, "they are coming! I see them coming now . . . the armed men . . ."

"Listen to me, Konia," said Perique. "Take your hand away from my arm, please."

She stood back from him a little.

"And never touch me again," said Perique.

"My lord, I am sorry," said the girl. "But you can see that my hands are clean."

"And that's the trouble, Konia," he said. "They're clean, and so are you. Don't try to understand what I say, but never touch me again."

"No, my lord," said the girl, bewildered. And then she whispered, "They are here! They are here!"

"I can hear the heels clicking," said Perique, "and I can feel the weight of the guns. Hot weather, Konia, for all that iron junk to be carted around."

He turned his head and saw six men with rifles coming straight up to him. The captain of the constabulary walked in advance of the others to make the arrest. And in the offing, sauntering with his hands in his pockets, was Ellis, the lucky captain of the *Nancy Lee*. He wore a grin on his big, brown face, and there was a satisfied twinkling in his eyes.

The captain stopped, shrugged his shoulders, and took a panting breath. "Are you James Parry?" he asked.

"That's my name," said Perique.

"You are under arrest," said the captain.

"Am I?" asked Perique.

"Take him, men," said the captain.

They stepped forward. All of them were specimens of the "dirty white" which has been described before.

"All right, boys," said Perique. "Don't trouble yourselves to touch me, though. You can see for yourselves that I'm taken, as my friend the captain says. Now that I'm taken, captain, suppose you tell me what's the charge?"

The captain was a little worried. He had a short bit of mustache on his upper lip and he managed to twist that lip, now, so that he was able to bite the edge of the mustache.

"I'm glad that you take this so easily, Parry," he said. "You'll take it less easily when you hear the charge. The murder of Harrison Lee of the ship *Nancy Lee*. We want you for that, Parry."

"Ah? Murder?" said Perique. "Konia, give me one of those cigarettes."

The girl opened the box, let him select one, and lighted a match for him. She did these things with a serious face of concern, as though she were afraid that she might go through the ceremony in the wrong way.

"Murder?" said Perique, breathing out clouds of smoke. "I didn't murder poor Harry Lee. I only saw him once in my life."

"Once might be enough," said the captain. "I warn you

31

that what you say may appear as King's evidence later on. But do you care to state exactly what happened on the one occasion when you admit you were with Harrison Lee?"

"You ought to be a lawyer, captain," said Perique. "You have the formal lingo perfectly. Sit down, if there's a chair. No chair? Then perhaps you can take it standing."

"This insolence will not get you farther forward," said the captain.

"No insolence in the world," said Perique. "Nothing but facts, my dear captain. It was on the beach at Vanua, at the place Joe Fitzpatrick runs. D'you know it?"

"I do not," said the captain tersely.

"That's a pity," said Perique. "He has the best brand of palm tree gin in the world."

"I'm talking to you about Harrison Lee and murder, Parry, not about palm tree gin."

"How long ago was it?"

"Three weeks."

"In Vanua, you say?"

"That's right. At Joe Fitzpatrick's place. Harry Lee had been doing a bit of drinking. Gin and milk sounds like baby food, but the dynamite's in it, just the same."

"I'm not here to waste the government's time on trifles, Mr. Parry," said the captain.

"So when Harry Lee sat in at a poker game with me and a few others," said Perique, "he lost his shirt in a few moments. That is to say, I actually let his coat stand for ten dollars when he was cleaned out; and so the coat went to me."

"Ah!" said the captain sharply. "His coat? You admit having his coat?"

"Certainly," said Perique. "After I saw that he was broke, I offered it back to him; but he was turning a bit sour. He said the coat had been damned bad luck to him, anyway. After he was gone, I saw that the sleeve had been torn. The coat wasn't worth two dollars, let alone ten. But I wore it

32

when I came over here from Vanua with old Kamakau on his outrigger."

"This makes an interesting story," said the captain, sneering. "I suppose you have confirmation?"

"Look behind you and you'll see it," said Perique. "There's Archie Ellis that was sitting in at that same poker game in Fitzpatrick's place at Vanua. You remember all the details, Archie, don't you?"

The grinning was stricken from the face of Ellis.

"What?" he exclaimed.

"You heard me, didn't you?" ran on Perique in his soothing, deep, soft-flowing voice. "Ellis is the fellow that Kamakau picked out of the sea with his outrigger; that's how I got to know the captain of the *Nancy Lee,* though. Back there in Vanua."

The captain said, frowning, "What is this, Captain Ellis? Is it true? Were you present when this poker game took place?"

Ellis was busy lighting a cigarette, his face contorted and darkened by the business, as it seemed. Now he straightened, blew forth smoke, and finally said:

"All right. I was there."

"You were there?" echoed the captain.

"Yes," said Ellis. "The story's straight."

The captain took a breath in through his teeth. His mouth twitched far to the side. Then he shrugged his shoulders.

"Very well," he said. "The thing must rest at that. Mr. Parry, I regret that we have disturbed you, but a report came . . ."

"Women will always be chattering, won't they?" murmured Perique.

The captain flushed. "Good day, Mr. Parry," he said.

"Sorry not to rise," said Perique, "but you know what a hammock is . . . terribly sorry that you didn't find a chair. Good-by, captain."

To these last remarks, the captain of the constabulary returned not a word of answer. He went stalking stiffly away, and even the back of his neck was red with his anger.

The officers who had followed him up the hill went slouching away behind their commander, and Perique wriggled himself into a more comfortable position.

Big Archibald Ellis stalked up to him and shook a fist in his face.

"You damned four-flusher!" he said. "How in hell did you dare to drag me in to—"

Perique caught the threatening fist in his hand with a light gesture. He held onto that hand as he said, "You can see how it is, Ellis. They think that I killed Harry Lee because I have his coat."

"I think you killed him myself," said Ellis, "and I . . . Let go of my hand, damn you!"

He put out his other hand to tear the fist out of the grasp of Perique, but the second hand was gripped also. Perique was saying:

"Don't we need one another, Ellis? I mean to say, the coat of Harry Lee rather ties me up with him. And the fact that you weren't picked out of the sea by Kamakau's boat is a stickler for you to get around. You only have me for witness, eh?"

Ellis, breathing hard, said nothing.

"You understand?" said Perique.

"Let me go. You're smashing the bones of my hands!" said Ellis. "Damn you, you . . ."

"You understand?" said Perique.

"I understand," said Ellis.

Perique let the hands go. They were ivory white where the pressure of that grasp had been squeezing; and at the tips of the fingers there was a swollen purple-red so that it seemed the blood was about to burst from the nails.

Ellis chafed his hands slowly together. "I'll see you again before very long; make yourself damned sure of that," he said.

"I'm even surer of you than I am of being damned," said Perique. "Have to rush away? Sorry, Ellis. I'll be seeing you soon, as you say."

Ellis, backing off a step or two, was so enraged by this polite tormenting that he thrust a hand suddenly back inside his coat.

"No, don't pull a gun," said Perique, "or my little girl, yonder, will slide her knife into you."

Ellis, jerking his head around, saw Konia standing straight, with her chin thrusting up into the air a little, and one hand pressed very close to her side, well muffled in the fullness of her skirt. The gleam of the knife looked out with only one small cat's-eye. But that was enough for Ellis.

Electric shudders of cold ran through his blood.

Perique was saying: "Have you met her, Ellis? Pretty little thing, isn't she? She's Konia. Nice name, isn't it? She's my foster child, or niece, or adopted cousin, or something or other. Don't you want to meet her? Well, good-by, Ellis. Be seeing you!"

Konia was staring fixedly at Perique.

"Are you going to get some of those dresses I spoke about, Konia?" he asked.

"Yes, lord," said the girl. She bowed, and began to move backward from him.

"Wait a moment, Konia. Do you ever smoke?"

"Yes, lord."

"Take one of those cigarettes and light it."

She obeyed. She breathed out the smoke.

"Lift your head a little higher," said Perique.

She obeyed.

"Now turn more towards the sun. If it hurts your eyes, you can close them. There, that's better. That's better than better. That's perfect. What are you smiling about, Konia?"

"It is the warmth . . . of the sun, lord," said Konia.

"It makes you smile?"

"Yes, lord."

35

"Konia, you are an immense liar."

"Yes, lord," she said.

"Why do you carry such a long knife, Konia?"

"Because the blue of the steel is so pretty, lord."

"About the dresses, Konia . . . they can wait."

"Yes, lord," she said.

CHAPTER 7

Bill Smith came oozing into the presence of Perique, later on. Bill was always having a black spot of perspiration appear between his shoulder blades. A sort of sweet savor came from Bill, as of fruit stewing, or yams cooking with sugar cane; perhaps it was the natural aroma of Bill Smith, frying in the fumes of an ocean of alcohol.

Konia brought him a canvas chair and adjusted it after measuring him with a glance. Bill Smith, sinking back into the chair, said to Perique: "You see what kind of a girl I found for you? She could get a job with a tailor. She could cut a suit of clothes to measure after she gave you one look. Look the way she fixes this chair for me. Better than I could do it myself. That's the kind of a wife I furnish for you, Mr. Parry."

"She's not a wife," said Perique. "She's a housekeeper. The hill is too far from the sea for her. The air is wrong. . . . She stays in her father's house and comes up here every day to look after things."

"I've seen 'em high and I've seen 'em low," said Bill Smith. "But I've never seen one like you, sir. I come over to tell you what's in the air."

"Tell me, then. Konia, start a breeze with that fan, will you?"

Konia picked up the big three-foot fan of braided palm leaves and began to sway it; the air puffed softly over the two men.

Bill Smith said: "There's a noise around Tupia that you're a taboo with the natives and that you've got a name that people would know better than they know James Parry."

Bill Smith waited, but Perique said nothing. Finally Smith went on: "The captain of the constabulary swears that you're a crook and that you've wriggled out of being hanged for the killing of Harrison Lee by scaring Ellis into testifying for you. And now Matthew Coffee is asking you to come over for dinner and high jinks this evening.

"Coffee has the house right there across the little gorge. You could throw a stone into it from your barred window, yonder."

"If I go to Coffee's house tonight, do you think they'll try to frame me?" asked Perique.

"What else would they try to do?"

"They've sent a racing outrigger down the wind to Kandava and one of Coffee's men is on board her. He's to go ashore, describe you, and see if he can get hold of any sort of a grip for the law when it wants to put its hand on you."

"How do you know all these things, Smith?" asked Perique.

"I gotta have ears working for me day and night," said Bill Smith. "Besides, I like to see one gentleman play his hand against a whole table of trouble, and make his draw with the rest, and try to win."

"What chance have I, Bill?"

"The chance? One in a thousand. The girl wants you put away. I mean, Nancy Lee wants you put away, and Nancy is the girl that nobody stops on this island."

"Why not?" asked Perique.

"She's got a way about her, is all I can say. I'll tell you what kind of a way she's got. When the men fall in love with Nancy Lee, the other womenfolk and wives don't even get jealous of her. They just set back and laugh. Everybody that comes to Lanua falls in love with her. It's the regular rule. But it never amounts to anything. Except that all the gents that have got dizzy laugh a spell at themselves afterwards—and they're all ready to go out and die for Nancy Lee."

"How old is this girl?" asked Perique.

"Twenty-one or two . . . I don't know. She's been the queen since she was fifteen, sixteen."

"They're asking me tonight to the high jinks so that all the whites can look me over. Is that it?" asked Perique.

"Aye, and maybe to frame you on the spot. Here comes a boy with the uniform of Matthew Coffee's house servants; that green cloak worn so short, and the flat straw hat with the feather in it. Coffee knows how to put the dog on his servants. The king of England is pretty far away, but the king of Lanua is Matthew Coffee, in spite of any governor that may happen to be on the spot."

The man came up to Perique and made his salutation with a good deal of natural courtesy and grace; then he presented a letter.

"Open it up and read it for me, Bill, will you?" asked Perique.

The hungry hand of Bill Smith instantly had the letter open, and he was reading aloud:

My dear Mr. James Parry:

It has not been my pleasure to meet you but the white people on Lanua are so few that we look upon one another as club members, so to speak, and we do away with most of the formalities. Won't you come to dine with me? The time: half an hour before sunset, or thereabouts.

Cordially yours,

Matthew Coffee.

Perique waved his hand at the boy and said in the native dialect: "Tell your master that I'm very grateful to him and

38

that nothing could keep me from accepting his kind invitation. I shall be at his house tonight."

The boy went off at once. Bill Smith was staring helplessly. Konia stopped swinging the fan to exclaim: "You may go alive, but you never will come back alive!"

"Well," said Perique, "I want a chance to have a little chat with the green-eyed girl, Nancy Lee, and where shall I see her except at the house of Coffee?"

"She won't be there," said Bill Smith. "She's got a dead father to mourn about; she won't be out to dinner."

"A girl with a pair of eyes as green as those," said Perique, "will get a slice of revenge first and try the flavor of it in her cup of mourning and tears and all that. Don't argue with me, Konia.

"Don't argue, Bill. It's too hot for a lot of talking.

"Bill, have somebody bring me half a siphon of soda with a pint of gin poured into it, will you?"

The hour was set for half an hour before sunset, but no one with a knowledge of manners in the tropics would dream of coming until half an hour after dark.

It was at this time that people began to swarm toward the big house of Matthew Coffee, which stood on the side of the narrow gorge opposite the tavern of Bill Smith.

The warehouses and the offices of Coffee and Coffee, that celebrated old firm, spread out over the much lower ground toward Tupia Beach. These buildings stood about a sort of compound as it might be called, for the buildings were contiguous and outlined an uneven space of ground, a sort of rambling court.

Between the corners of the buildings were sections of heavy palisade. The sharp points of the stakes threatened to impale any adventurous thieves; and in addition, there was a liberal scattering of barbed wire and of sharp fragments of broken bottles that extended all along the top of the palisade, imbedded in a sheathing of shallow, strong cement.

This protection was so sufficient that Coffee maintained only one night watchman.

This was a fellow of mixed Lanuan and European blood, called Jackie for first name and last. He carried on his simple rounds of the yard a number ten shotgun, with the two barrels sawed off and filled with heavy charges of buckshot, a handful to each barrel. He had a knife and a revolver, also; and the native blood showed particularly in his favorite weapon, which was a knobby little club that he wore at his belt.

Jackie at the particular moment, perhaps ten minutes after the sun had dipped and the green of the brief twilight had rimmed the horizon before the stars came showering down —Jackie at this moment, a little later, was cupping his hands before his eyes and staring at a light which he could see inside the office of the head of the firm, the office of Matthew Coffee himself.

There was a man in there who kept in a fixed position behind a desk, so that all Jackie could see was the hands, yellowish white from exposure to the sun, and very strongly made. Those hands stirred only slightly, but every stir brought a new flash of light from the thing that was held between the double palms.

Jackie would have sworn that it was as big as a pigeon's egg, the first moment that he glanced at it. Before the end, it seemed to him a pearl huger than a hen's egg. It contained all the light of a full, round moon, it seemed to Jackie. All the stars of the heavens—even all the lucky ones—rolled together would not have made a luminary as brilliant as the huge pearl which was being turned slightly, shifting up and down between those double palms.

The light went out. The puff of breath that extinguished the lamp seemed to Jackie like the stroke of a great dark wing, but though the pearl no longer could be seen, for some moments Jackie remained at the corner of the buildings with a dazzled brain. As though he had been looking at the fiery sun, he still could see the image of that mighty pearl, now in dazzling moon-white, now in crimson that stared into and hurt the eyes.

Jackie's mind went wandering far afield.

He could see the ship that carried the great pearl away in state, bound for some foreign ruler. He could see the pearl shine as the topmost jewel in the crown of an emperor.

And yet this pearl was only a single treasure in the old-fashioned little safe of Coffee and Coffee!

Well, all the natives of the island knew that Matthew Coffee had exchanged the happiness of his soul for the sake of riches in this round, green, beautiful world. If the treasures were as marvelous as the huge pearl, Jackie knew that Matthew Coffee had struck a bargain.

The lungs of Jackie began to burn, as though all the labors of a thousand generations of pearl divers were now consuming him.

Jackie had stood in this trance for some time. And so deep was his preoccupation that he did not see the shadowy figure that slipped up the side of the wall behind him. All the premonitory warning that Jackie felt was a slight tugging at his belt.

He returned in time to receive between the eyes a crushing blow delivered with his own short-handled club.

Jackie fell upon his knees. He was one of the few Christianized natives on the island.

That was why his words, that came in a whisper from his stunned brain and body, were: "I'm only poor Jackie . . . ah, heaven receive my soul gently!"

The second blow fell and dashed out his brains.

CHAPTER 8

It was something like fifteen or twenty minutes afterward that big Perique came striding up to the entrance gate of Matthew Coffee. A white-clad pair of officers of the con-

41

stabulary of Lanua were stationed just inside that gate and gave a sort of public importance and sanction to the affair.

When they saw Perique, they did not ask his name, but saluted. He recognized two of the "dirty whites" who had followed their captain up the hill this day to arrest James Parry. Perique, however, did not smile as he walked on up the drive toward the lighted face of the house. There was so much light, in fact, that when he looked down at his right sleeve, he was able to see the little patch above the wristband.

The sight of this patch made him set his teeth a little. He looked up suddenly, and it seemed to him that above the tips of the enormous palms the stars were all rushing in a great pool, around and around, drawn toward a vortex.

Something would happen on this night. A great, great deal would happen. Perhaps in this house, perhaps after the arrival of the mail steamer from Kandava.

Would they have found anyone in Kandava who knew Perique by description? Well, they *ought* to be able to find someone . . . someone who could recall him in letters of burning red.

A moment later he was in the first court of the house of Matthew Coffee. For it was built after a sort of Pompeian style, a series of spreading courts surrounded by wooden instead of stone pillars, but giving an air of indescribable space and coolness to the place.

In the middle of the central court a stream of water from the spring was forced up high in the air by the work of half a dozen laborers who toiled in the underground room at the roots of the spring.

Their grunting and straining could not be seen, but the fair shining of the fountain and the whisper of it through the air was enough to fill the minds of the guests. The moon was up, silvering the top tip of that tossing fountain spray. This was the central eye which shone out an invitation to happiness to all the guests of Matthew Coffee.

Coffee himself moved here and there to see that things were

started well. And after a moment he came to Perique, who strode head-high above the other guests.

Coffee went straight up to him and said, "This is a happiness, Mr. Parry. Thank you for coming. I hope you'll be at home with us . . ."

All very pleasant words, but Perique noted that the eye of Matthew Coffee had fixed upon the right sleeve of the white duck coat—fixed on it at the very point where the duck was torn and had been patched neatly over by a clever needle.

"And I want you to meet a friend of mine . . . What am I saying?" went on Coffee cordially. "The friend of all of us, I should say. Ah, here she is. Nancy, come here a moment, will you? This is the new man on Lanua. This is Mr. James Parry. Miss Nancy Lee! Take care of him, Nancy, while I look after some of the others."

That was how they were stranded together in the midst of the crowd. Perhaps there were fifty or sixty people in the house of Matthew Coffee, and more were coming. And every one of them, man or woman, already had heard about Perique. He felt and saw on every hand the flash of eyes bright with hostility. On the whole they looked a bit cleaner than the usual group one can find on a small island in the South Seas. The men were not so brandy-bloated and the women were dressed with more pride.

Perhaps that difference could be charged largely to the girl who was beside him.

Still she was not in mourning for her dead father. Perhaps she never would be in mourning so far as clothes or lip service were concerned. But a stern brightness about the eyes indicated that there was a fire in her that could not easily be extinguished, and Parry would have sworn that he knew what that fire was.

She had dedicated herself to bringing justice upon the murderer, if murder it had been, and she would not stop working to waken justice and bring it on the heels of the guilty. And here, before her, was the man who wore the coat

43

of the dead man!

She was wearing a white dress of some light, windy stuff, like tulle, and this girlish lightness of costume exaggerated the slender smoothness of her arms and throat. She looked more like a child than a woman, except that her face was refined and matured. Those sea-green eyes held steadily on big Perique.

He said, "We've got to talk to each other. Suppose that we go over there where the lights are not so bright. Will you do that?"

She went beside him without saying a word. She walked well, without the stultified, stumping step of most women, and so he knew that she had all her inches without the use of high heels. It was a free, light stride; she would be able to run well, too; the sunny bronze of her skin, so dark against the white of the dress, had not been built up by lying on the beach, but by running, swimming, rowing in the open.

The place to which he took her was at the side of the second court where there was a raised terrace, set off with a couple of young palm trees and covered with shaven lawn. From this high point they could look over the wall of the garden on the opposite side and so down the shadows of a long valley into the bay, where the moonlit water seemed to be rising in a great wall, ready to flow inland and wash about their feet. The trade wind was now obscuring the center of the bay, but along the shore where the heights cut away the strength of the breeze, there was a smooth stretch that took the dappling of the stars.

"This is a good place," said Perique. "This is far enough away from the drinks so that other people won't bother us much. Now you can say what you please."

"What do you think I'm going to say?" she said.

"You want to know where I got this coat," said Perique.

"I know that. At a poker game," said the girl. "The whole town of Tupia knows how you got it."

"And *you* know that I didn't?"

44

"I think I know you didn't," said the girl.

"If I didn't get the coat that way, I must have got it by foul play?"

Here she turned a little more toward him and looked for a long time at his face. It was not hard for women to look at Perique because he was a handsome fellow and he knew it; but he never before had been regarded with such a scrutiny as this. It was as though a pair of clear mirrors were catching strong beams of light and throwing them through the windows of his soul, searching everything inside him. He became aware, suddenly, that his nose was not altogether straight— having been broken a couple of times—and that the left side of his upper lip was slightly thickened and drooping, because it had been cut cleanly open against his teeth, on a day, or rather upon a night.

In this way Perique began to see himself anew. Detail by detail, the features stood out before him and he saw a fellow magnificent, perhaps, but a bit brutal. Above all, he used his eyes as others did not, moving them slowly, letting them linger boldly on everything that he wished to consider.

He said, "Go ahead and make the survey, and take your time. I'm doing the same."

But though he smiled, the smile was an affectation.

She said, "If you're honest, you won't be nervous, will you?"

"I don't know," said Perique. "I have never had anyone glint the old green lightning through me the way you're doing. I've never been turned into a small boy since I was in short pants."

"I wish you'd tell me about yourself," said the girl.

"I'm glad to. Every man likes to talk about himself," said Perique. "I'm about twenty-seven years old. I've been to school. Now I'm in the South Seas for my health, and I find the climate pretty good; don't you?"

"Have you any business?" she asked.

"Sometimes," said Perique. "I'm not particular."

45

"You're not particular?" she echoed.

"No, I'm not particular," he answered, defying her.

"You don't have to throw so much muscle into your attitude," said she. "I'm neither judge nor policeman. I can't *make* you talk to me if you don't want to."

"That's true," said Perique, "but I'm surprised that you realize it. You are used to melting everything in the old green fire and turning men into soft wax, and all that. You won't melt me."

"I can see that I won't," said the girl. "But isn't it being a little silly to be so defiant?"

"Defiant of a poor little helpless girl like you?" asked Perique.

"Those adjectives are your own, though," she replied.

"I'll tell you," said Perique. "You are more powerful than the governor and the silly captain of the constabulary. And you know it. This place is so small and you're so big in it that no man can stand against you. If you say the word, every man on the island will grab guns and make for me. You are the boss of the show."

"That doesn't need to frighten you," she replied.

"Why doesn't it? I'm not immortal."

"If the whites went for you, you could fade away into the interior, and the natives would take care of you as though you were a god, Perique."

He put out a hand. He had not meant to do that, but the name struck at him like a knife. His fingers closed on her arm, just at the elbow, and the force of his grip jerked her arm straight. He snatched his hand away.

"I'm sorry," said Perique. "I'm damned sorry. That was one of those instinctive reflexes. Dodging after the bullet has gone by, and that sort of thing."

"Is the name as bad as all that?" she asked.

"They're talking, are they?" asked Perique softly. "They're spreading it around?"

She looked at him closely.

46

"You're wrong," she said. "Get those ideas out of your mind. It was only Konia who talked to me."

"Konia?" exclaimed Perique. "Excuse me, but I don't believe that."

"You don't believe she'd talk?"

"I know she wouldn't."

"She came to ask me what sort of dresses she should buy," said the girl. "She said there was a man who didn't want people to be handling her with their eyes and he'd given her money to buy clothes. How much does Konia think about you?"

"Konia's a pretty little girl," said Perique. "And I'm just taking up a little of her spare time."

"Is she in love with you?" asked Nancy Lee.

"Certainly not," said Perique. "I thought it would be as well if she slipped a frock on. You know."

"I know," agreed Nancy Lee. "I saw a yearling thoroughbred once. A filly. Next to that yearling, Konia is the most beautiful thing that ever danced. Sometimes her nakedness doesn't matter; it's like a goddess being free in the air; but sometimes it *does* matter, when there is too much palm tree gin in the brains of the men. Is that what you mean?"

"That's what I mean," said Perique. "She talked to you, I see."

"She said you did a good deal of drinking. And then you sent her home to get dressed."

"After that, she told you my name."

"She tells me everything," said Nancy Lee.

"Does she?"

"That is, she did until today. She will never tell me any secrets after this. When the name slipped from her, she was in an agony. She—"

"I don't want to hear about it," said Perique.

"Don't you?"

"No, if you please."

The girl sighed. She sat down in one of the canvas chairs

47

and Perique took a chair beside her.

"What does the name mean, after all?" asked Nancy Lee.

"You'll find out when the mail boat comes in from Kandava," said Perique.

"There were no inquiries about Perique. The questions were sent over about one James Parry."

"Wait a moment. I want to follow that. You knew the nickname in time to send it over to Kandava . . . and you didn't?"

"No."

"You didn't even open up that name and ask among the traders and the white trash here in Tupia?"

"No."

Perique lighted a cigarette. His mouth was too dry. All at once he needed a drink.

"It was because Konia just let the name slip . . . that's why you wouldn't use it?"

"That was only being decent," said Nancy Lee.

"But women never are decent. They never give up an advantage. They cut throats—in the dark," muttered Perique.

"Did Perique ever cut a throat in the dark?" she asked.

"You'll hear about Perique one day," he said. "What do you think I'll tell you about that beachcomber in his bare feet, with a knife between his teeth and his belly full of rum?"

"All right, don't tell me," she answered. "Will you tell me one thing? Did you, on your honor, have anything to do with the death of my father?"

"Will you believe what I tell you?"

"Yes."

"Then you're a little cracked," said he. "Never believe a damned thing that Perique tells you."

"I'm talking to James Parry," said the girl.

"Ah, are you?" he asked. "Well, perhaps. But that's why I'll answer no questions."

"You'll answer one, I hope. When you knew that the coat

48

was the giveaway, why did you wear it here tonight? You bought others today in Tupia."

"You know everything, don't you?"

"No; only as much as I can find out about you. Why did you come wearing that coat? Simply to let it shock me?"

"That was one reason," he said.

"When you passed me on the street, and I looked so hard at you, then you knew that there was something wrong," she interpreted. "Afterward, you heard some talk about me. Perhaps you even heard that I'm well known in Tupia. You told yourself that you wouldn't be run off the island of Lanua by any girl. If she didn't like anything about you, she could go hang. If you had her father's coat, why, you'd wear it on purpose, before her eyes."

He threw the cigarette on the ground and stamped on it. Smoke still was fuming from his nostrils into the moonlight.

"That's the way Perique would reason—not James Parry," said the girl. "Have I any hold on you?"

"That's what I said you'd never have. You have a hold on everybody else in the island . . . all the whites, anyway. I laughed to myself and said that green eyes and all, you would never have a grip on me, not even the purchase of a fingerhold. But in spite of me, now you have it. No, damn it. You *have* no hold."

She was smoothing her arm at the elbow with a thoughtful hand.

He jerked out, suddenly: "When I caught you by the arm —did I hurt you?"

"No," said the girl.

"I did," said Perique. "I hurt you."

"No," she answered, shaking her head.

"I did. In the morning it will be black and blue."

"No," she said. "It's all right."

"On your honor?" he asked.

She said nothing, at that.

"Damn!" said Perique.

49

"I'll wear long sleeves until there's not a mark," said Nancy Lee. "Nobody shall know. Will you talk to me about Konia?"

"No. I'm through talking," said Perique.

"You know," said the girl, "that the information Kandava sends about James Parry may not mean very much. But the moment a whisper goes abroad that you are Perique . . . that, plus the suspicion about my father's death . . . what would they do with you?"

"They'd hang me to the nearest tree."

"Yes, I think they really would . . . Isn't that a point for bargaining?"

"Go ahead, then."

Here they could hear the voice of the host saying jovially, "Hello, Kialia! Hello! You didn't put the keys in these trousers, and we can't open the wine cellar now. Find the keys and bring them out, will you? You'll have us all dying of thirst, Kialia!"

The girl said, "Konia will marry you . . . not a Christian marriage, but just one of those native affairs. Pick her up and carry her over your threshold. Or even without that much formality, she'll follow you. Is that true?"

"No," said Perique. "We'd better not talk about her."

"Are you afraid?" asked the girl.

Slowly he sank back into the chair.

She went on, "You've sent her away. When she comes back, send her away again."

She waited. Perique said nothing.

"Just the sending won't be enough. You'll have to be cruel to her . . . You will have to call her a mongrel—a yellow dog . . . you'll have to make her hate you, or else she'll keep on loving you."

Perique lighted another cigarette. He breathed out the smoke through his nostrils only.

"You see how it is," said Nancy Lee. "When Konia makes up her mind to fall in love, nobody can resist her; and she's made up her mind. There's a beachcomber called Perique

50

who would take her in a moment. The same beachcomber may have murdered Harrison Lee. But the gentleman named James Parry is able to do the right thing."

"Stop, will you?" said Perique. "I want to think."

"Let me do it for you," said the girl. "Thinking won't help. Konia will come dancing and singing back to you the moment you leave it all to thinking."

"I never heard anything like her singing," remembered Perique. "The sun was on her throat. There was a pulse of gold in the hollow of it."

"A man like James Parry," said the girl, "is able to reason everything out to the end. A fellow such as Perique would never trouble about reasoning. He'd take his pleasure where he found it, and lie in the sun. But you know what the story of Konia would be. All those stories are the same.

"Then the man goes away from the girl and the children and all. Or else he stays and rots like seaweed on the beach. It's a tragedy either way. In the end he grows hungry for a girl of his own kind. He wants to go home and be clean. You know how it always goes."

She made a gesture with both hands and smiled at him. The whole blond, shining beauty of the northern lands seemed to hold out its arms.

Perique looked off across Tupia Bay.

"All right," he said.

She stood up.

"I know you'll do what I say," she said. "And not a syllable about that beachcomber, Perique, shall ever pass my lips; none that will connect him with you, at any rate."

Perique held out his hand.

She looked down at it and then up at his face.

"There's another way to put things," she said.

He stared at the hand she had refused and then put it into a pocket.

"Go ahead," he answered.

"I think that Perique killed Harrison Lee," she said, "and

I hope he hangs for it! I'm going to help hang him if I can!"

He watched her silently and then made a little gesture as though offering her the way past him.

She went down the slope of the lawn. She entered the brightness of the lights. People suddenly spilled out around her. There was a handsome lad as brown as an islander who caught hold of her. Waltz music was throbbing and yearning in the air. The lad whirled her away over the lawn. She seemed between helpless laughter and a protest, but she was dancing beautifully.

"Ah, hell," said Perique.

He stretched himself. He could feel the robe of muscles pull and tingle against the bones, from his toes to the nape of his neck, to his fingers. He opened his hands and shut them into fists.

CHAPTER 9

There was serious concern in the voice and the manner of Matthew Coffee. As he explained to the governor, "None of the boys in my house are thieves. I'd trust any of 'em with anything. But the fact is that my keys are gone. Damned inconvenient. We'll have to smash open the door of the cellar with axes. Didn't have any liquor upstairs except what was in the cooling room."

The Honorable Governor Irvine Glastonbury touched his damp forehead with his handkerchief.

"Rotten luck, Matthew," he said. "But a man must drink, what? No way of polishing up the old room and trimming the wicks of the stars except by using a bit of punch, from time to time, eh? But don't you trust these bally servants of yours. Never trust an islander, Matthew. Great Gad, no! I wouldn't dream of it. The foot in the face. That's the only policy."

"Not so loud, Irvine! Not so infernally loud," said Matthew Coffee, shaking his massive head. "Some of these people may hear you and talk—talk enough to have it come to the ears of the natives—and then our happy days would be over. Here, boy. Take the ax and smash in the cellar door. That's the only thing that we can do. Infernally strange. Well, maybe one of the lads is a rascal."

"Governor Glastonbury . . ."

"My dear Nancy Lee. Will you dance this with me?"

"I'd rather talk it with you, because I've been hearing stories."

"You tell me about everything, and I'll give you the truth."

"Did you ever hear of a fellow called Perique?"

"Perique? Oh, they've started that old legend, have they?" laughed the governor. "Dear Nancy, you ought to know that there never was a real Perique—never at all! He's just one of the old South Seas legends!"

"Oh, he's old, is he?" asked Nancy Lee.

"I've been hearing about him for twenty years, I suppose. Won't you dance this, Nancy?"

"I'd love to, but—I can't, because—don't forget me later, Governor Glastonbury. Mr. Coffee! Did you hear what the governor was saying?"

"I didn't, Nancy. I was wondering about my infernal keys. One of the confounded boys in my house must have stolen them. I'll have the hide off the fellow's back if I catch him . . . have had to smash in the cellar door, you see? What was it about, Nancy?"

"About an old South Sea legend—a man called Perique."

"Legend? Legend?" said Matthew Coffee. "There's no legend about Perique."

"Then even the *story* doesn't exist?"

"Of course it does. And so does the man. Perique! He's the one who killed the three men in the knife fight on the beach somewhere. He's the fellow who sailed the old ketch *Harmony* through the Chisholm Reefs, single-handed. Ever see Chisholm Reefs?"

"I've seen them. They're like a maelstrom. How could one man do such a thing? It's not possible for one pair of hands . . ."

"Perique is always two . . . himself and the devil. Yes, he sailed the *Harmony* through the reefs, right enough. I know, because I talked afterward with Captain Malcolm Wallace of the King's cutter *Clovelly*. He was chasing Perique. He didn't quite dare to try the passage of the reefs, even with his ship fully manned with picked sailors, but he slid the cutter around inside the reef in time to see a boat putting off from the *Harmony* with only a single man in it. And when they boarded the *Harmony* itself, there was not a soul on board."

"That's a story to remember," said the girl. "A man who could do such things—it's queer that more people don't know him."

"A good many who've seen him have died suddenly on the spot."

"What's the look of him?"

"Thirty-five or forty—huge fellow—only a few inches under seven feet—terrible scar across his upper lip and cheek—hair growing down over the first joints of his fingers."

He broke off to say, "Why are you smiling?"

"I was just thinking that it's like the description of an ogre out of a fairy tale."

"Perique is enough of an ogre. Stops at nothing. Kill a woman as soon as he'd kill a man. Likes to kill with his hands. That's the beastly part of the brute. With his bare hands throttles the victims. Or else, with a club, beats out the brains. Strangling or braining with a club. Those are the usual marks of Perique."

"I'm going to remember," said the girl.

She went off through a jolly group and singled out her next man with, "Captain Singleton, I've been hearing a wild fairy tale."

"You come over here and let papa comfort you, poor dear,"

said Singleton.

"It's about that man-monster, that night-killer, that were-wolf, that Perique," said the girl.

"Oh, Perique? They do tell some wild yarns about him. But Perique's all right."

"Is he? Do you know him?"

"No. But a good friend of mine sailed with him."

"And wasn't murdered?"

"Perique's simply a big, lazy, good-natured beachcomber— one of a type—one of thousands who are all alike. That's all there is to him. Generous devil, they say. Give you the shirt off his back—he saved my friend from the sharks in handsome style, let me tell you. One of the dirty devils came so close that it raked some of the skin off the leg of my friend with its shaggy hide—but Perique got him away."

"Why, he must be a splendid fellow!" cried Nancy Lee.

"Yes—except in a poker game," said Singleton, smiling. "Watch the rascal in a poker game, my friend says—and never hold a gun under his nose."

"What do you mean by that?"

"Some people don't like force," said Singleton. "They won't stand compulsion. They hate marching orders. This Perique is a fellow of that type."

"But all the yarns about murder and such—"

"Rot, Nancy. All rot. I don't mean that there may not be some dead men in his past. But Perique's too good-natured for murder."

"Ah, is he? Good-natured?" murmured Nancy Lee thoughtfully.

And she shrugged her shoulders as though to let that part of the story slip away from her mind.

A tall man with a grave face came through the crowd, calling out in a louder and louder voice, "Is Wilshire of the constabulary here anywhere? Is Captain Wilshire here? Wilshire of the constabulary anywhere about . . ."

The voice was swallowed up. Captain Wilshire of the

constabulary was suddenly seen on the half run to get from the house. The murmur grew in volume and distinctness behind him.

"A horrible affair down at the Coffee offices. Attempt to rob the safe—night watchman murdered—brains dashed out with a club—and Captain Ellis, late of the ship *Nancy Lee*, found crushed to death under the safe, which had fallen from the wall."

CHAPTER 10

They went down with a sort of greedy, indecent haste. Perhaps, ideally, Captain Wilshire of the constabulary should have done the thing by himself, but Tupia society was not like that. It went in for things in a communal way, so that was the reason that twenty men, most of them white, or more or less white, went trailing down from the freshness of Tupia Hill into the muggier heat of the lowlands where the offices of Coffee and Coffee were located.

A constabulary officer leaned on his rifle beside a lantern on the ground as though he were illumining himself as a target for all concerned. But when the people came closer, they could see that the lantern light shone on another figure on the ground. The dead man had a smashed skull. The upper part of his face was gone.

Matthew Coffee had a dry sense of humor which could be sufficiently horrible at times. He said, "Jackie seems to have been killed by a blow delivered by some blunt instrument."

Then he turned his back and went on into the offices. The others trailed along behind him. They got to the innermost office of all, the Coffee sanctum, where the lieutenant of constabulary was shining forth in his white uniform, and Coffee's secretary, one Stephen Gregory, was also on guard.

A second dead man lay on the floor with his chest caved in. Above him, in the face of the wall, there was a gaping cavity with the ends of heavy bolts thrusting into it. Below this cavity stood the safe which once had filled it. There was a reeking stroke of red across the top of the safe, whose door was open. A snow of papers had drifted across the floor.

Everyone held back at the door of the office or, pressing through, lined up close to the wall. When the draft raised one of the flat papers and blew it against the feet of a man, he jumped as though he had been touched by a plague.

Matthew Coffee walked forward over the wreckage with an unconcerned face. He said, "Well, lieutenant, how did this all happen?"

"It's an easy thing to say how the job was done, but not so easy to find out who did it," said the officer. "Two people must have had in mind robbing the safe, Mr. Coffee. One of them was your captain, Ellis—and he lies there, now. But another man, or men, I should say, had been here before him. You can see what happened. The first fellow had determined to steal away the entire safe and open it at his pleasure. He had worked the bolts loose. You can see the ends of them, up there. And while he was at work, getting the safe in such a condition that he was able to take it away —there must have been help with him to manage that job, of course—he heard Ellis coming into the office, and the first robbers manage to get out of the way. Ellis comes in. I dare say that it's Ellis who has the keys—"

"Keys? Keys?" said Matthew Coffee. "Ah," he added, more quietly. "I understand, then. That's what became of the keys. They weren't stolen by one of the boys at my house. They were stolen by poor Ellis!"

He turned about to the men who solemnly lined the side wall of the room.

Most of them kept their eyes, drawn irresistibly, upon the horror of the face of Ellis, frozen in a vast contortion as he died.

"When I was wanting to get into the cellar for more drinks, Ellis was being throttled down here so that he'd never drink again," said the sardonic merchant.

No one smiled. The lieutenant of constabulary went on, "Ellis unlocks the door. You can see the keys of the safe still sticking in it—extraordinary thing, Mr. Coffee, that you should put the keys to a valuable safe on the same ring with your house keys."

"I begin to see just how extraordinary it is," answered Coffee.

He lifted his eyes gravely to the lieutenant. One always suspected some sort of a grim joke in those yellow-stained eyes of the trader.

The lieutenant went on, "There's the devilish irony of this thing. You see what happened. The locked safe was perched up there on the wall perfectly secure. But then you see as the heavy door swung open it completely unbalanced the safe and allowed it to tip over. Ellis, at the very moment when he was reaching for the treasure—if there was a treasure inside—was crushed to death."

Coffee said suddenly, "Then the stuff is still here! Is that right, Gregory? The stuff wasn't taken out of the office at all?"

Stephen Gregory was a big beef of a man, never intended by nature for life in a tropical climate. He shook his head until the fat of his jowls quavered. He said, "That's the devil of it."

All the ease went out of the manner of Matthew Coffee. His voice had the snap and the ring of a barking dog.

"Do you mean they got at the pearls and cleaned them out, Gregory?"

"I'm sorry. I mean that."

Coffee went up to him and gripped his arm at the elbow.

"All the small stuff. They didn't get at the big fellow, did they?" He whispered, but everyone could hear the panting words.

Gregory said, "I'm sorry. They did."

"Damn your sorrow!" burst out Coffee. "I say, *damn your sorrow!*"

The words were not altogether to be unexpected from a man who had just suffered a considerable loss, and who, moreover, had looked on two dead men that night; but there was an excess of savage, snarling rage in the voice of Coffee that sent a shudder through the people who were listening there.

Coffee went right on, wheeling about and hurling the words at the lieutenant.

"Then your theory has a hole in it that I can drive a cart and horse through. The first robbers prepare the safe—at the last minute Ellis frightened them away. Ellis is killed by the fall of the safe—then how the devil did the loot escape?"

The lieutenant flushed! Again, the words that had been spoken were not so bad. It was the overplus of brutal anger and sneering suspicion which supercharged the voice of the trader.

Captain Wilshire came to the rescue of his subordinate.

"The thing's easily explained. The first gang fled into the next room, there. They waited, badly frightened because Ellis was in here. But when the safe fell and killed Captain Ellis, they naturally came back through this room. That was when they secured the loot."

Coffee stared at the captain and said, "Bah!"

Wilshire, firing up, said through his teeth, "I won't be talked to in this manner!"

"I can't understand you when you chew up your words in this manner," said Coffee. "But I never heard of a theory as childish as this. Robbers frightened from their work by a single man. Robbers skulking in an adjoining room—don't you suppose that Ellis would have had the brains to look into the rooms adjoining this one before he attempted to rob my safe?"

"I see, Mr. Coffee," said the captain, "that you insist upon

59

enlarging this robbery into a mystery. You are free to form as many theories as you please, of course."

Coffee said: "I would like to point out one thing, if I may be listened to: a double attempt is made to rob my safe on this night. Why should *two* such attempts be made? Because there was in that safe a pearl of enormous value, that was not there the day before. Now, I ask you, who committed the crime or the attempt? Only the men who knew that the pearl was there! Wait a moment. I want to ask who was first on the spot after the commission of the crime?"

"Mr. Gregory was the first here," said the lieutenant.

Coffee whirled about and faced Gregory. "Ah, is that so?" he asked. "I might have guessed that. First on the spot, were you, Gregory? First in the office, were you? Not drinking your usual rounds of gin, tonight? No, assiduous in your duty, for once? Bah!"

"I don't believe that I'll endure . . ." began the secretary.

But here Coffee cut in: "Be still, damn you! You're a liar and a thief, and I'll have it proved! I want all of you people to understand this business. You may think that I'm a little rough, but now I'll tell you why.

"You understand that Ellis, who lies dead there, only had brains for one thing—pearls! He knew every shallow in the South Pacific where pearls could be found or ever had been fished. That was why I backed him in the search. He was the pearl fisher; I was his financial backer.

"Poor dead Harry Lee was the real captain of the ship. He did the navigating and handled the crew—none better—and Ellis was the supernumerary, called captain of the ship because his pride wouldn't let him take any other place on it.

"Now, he'd made some fair voyages for me. Only fair. I'd told him before his last venture that this was the ultimate time he'd have my backing unless the returns were much larger than on previous occasions. The threat seemed to work.

"When Ellis was picked out of the sea by the outrigger, he

was carrying tied around his neck a small bag of pearls. Some of them were the ordinary run, such as Ellis had brought home before. But one of them was worthy of the crown of a king—worthy of being the central jewel of a king's crown, even if he were king of England! Ellis carried that pearl along with the rest on shore and then he showed them all to me in my office.

"He could hardly let the pearl go from his hands. That explains why he came to this office tonight to commit robbery. He'd been honest enough to show me the spoils of war. But when he began to dream about that pearl, the bigness of it and the shine of it filled his brain like a full moon.

"Now, my friends, I'm going to offer you another fact. The only other human being on Lanua Island who could have known of the existence of that pearl was the man who sees everything that goes into my safe. That man is my secretary, and a damned poor, drunken one he's been for the last year or two, always hungry to go home. That's Stephen Gregory. Gregory, stand out and confess that you're the thief!"

Gregory shouted with a sudden violence: "It's a lie! It's a lie!"

Coffee pointed his finger like a gun: "A lie that you knew that the pearl was in the safe?" he demanded.

"A lie that I would think of—"

"Bah, we all think of crime," said Coffee, "but most of us have brains enough not to do it. Look at his face, my friends! Did you ever see more guilt in any poor devil? Gregory, if you have any brains at all in your gin-stuffed head, you'll confess and restore the stuff. It will make everyone go easy with you!"

Gregory had raised a fist above his head as though he would dash it into the face of Coffee. He even made half a step forward while the trader stood sneering, undaunted.

And it was as though he had conquered by the sheer force of eye, alone. For Gregory, completing his stride, buckled at the knees. He pitched forward, struck the floor with great weight, and spilled over on his back.

He had knocked his face against the floor. Blood was running out of both nostrils. The red of it spluttered and sprayed out on his snoring breath. He looked like a dying man.

"Just go through his pockets," suggested Coffee. "He's only fainted—which is as good as a confession."

The lieutenant of constabulary already was on his knees. The very first thing that he drew out was a fat wallet which contained a thick sheaf of bills still in a brown paper wrapper as they had come from the bank. And written across the back of the wrapper in a rapid scrawl appeared the words "Coffee and Coffee."

"There!" said Matthew Coffee triumphantly. "I give you your criminal, Captain Wilshire. That's the hard cash he stole out of the safe. Search through the rest of his clothes and you'll find the pearl!"

They searched, but the pearl was not found as Gregory rallied from his fainting spell. At the same time the hoarse blast of a steamer's whistle came dimly roaring from the harbor. The mail steamer had arrived from Kandava.

CHAPTER 11

Murder, even a double murder, might interrupt a party at Tupia but could not end it. The garden of Matthew Coffee still was lighted, and people were drinking, laughing, dancing. Coffee himself had gone straight back to his house after his brief absence. The governor never had left the grounds, so that there always was a focal point about which the merriment could be gathered.

In the meantime, the *Flying Spray* had steamed into Tupia Harbor, blowing her whistle angrily, as though she were proceeding through a fog.

The explanation came when her boat came in beside the

pier and a savagely raging first mate climbed up the steps before the others.

Captain Wilshire's lieutenant of constabulary had rushed sweating down to the dock and on him fell the wrath of the mate.

"The light on Nihoni Point!" shouted the mate.

"What's the matter with it?" asked the lieutenant.

"There ain't any matter. There ain't any light!" roared the mate. "We almost come and smashed our nose on the reef inside the harbor. We had to feel our way in with a searchlight like a drunk stumbling up a flight of stairs. I never seen such a damn, poorly run island as Lanua, anyway. You ain't got the brains to keep a fire going. You leave the ships blind to come in off the sea. . . ."

The lieutenant did not even stay to argue the matter. If the light were out at Nihoni Point, God alone could tell what other ship might fail to fumble its way into the harbor of Tupia and be lost in the night. But old Tom Washburn was not a man to allow that light to dwindle, let alone permit it to go out. He had trimmed the lamps faithfully for a dozen years, living out there in the solitude of the point with no better company than his pipe and his fishlines.

He came to Tupia exactly once a month for a five-gallon jug of palm tree gin, which just lasted to keep his whistle wet for thirty days. The thirst of Tom Washburn was as regular as the motions of the moon.

Of all the men in the world, Tom Washburn was apt to be the last to fail in an appointed duty—so long as he had his regular ration of gin per day.

So the lieutenant got a horse and galloped it like mad all the way to Nihoni Point, along the curving, firm sand of the shore, and then over the low ridge of hills.

In the meantime, a noisy load of iron and brass junk was being rowed in from the *Flying Spray* and unloaded on the pier for the metal workers of Tupia, a godsend to them; and the passengers bound for Tupia made their way up the hill toward the heart of the old town.

The natives hated to work at this hour of the night, but a sufficient number of them had turned out to act as porters, packing enormous loads on their backs, and then running with amazing power up the slope. An islander often can work like five white men for half an hour. Afterward he has to take a long rest. But the men of Lanua were accustomed to the slope of that hill that climbed from the harbor level, and they went up it at a rush.

One of the men from Kandava wanted only a guide, however; he was calling out in a fairly smooth flow of dialect: "I want a guide to the captain of the constabulary. One of you boys know where I can find him?"

They knew, of course, better than they knew the palms of their hands, where the man of law was to be found; but his was a name they did not care to handle. Into his presence they did not wish to come, and there was no answer to the stocky, powerful fellow who kept on calling out.

He had a carry-all strapped like a knapsack behind his shoulders, and in his hand was a walking stick that had the rough dimensions of a club. He was a fellow who looked fit to take care of himself anywhere in a free-for-all.

A slender lad, tall, quick-moving, presently went past the man of the club and said over his shoulder: "Follow me to the captain!"

He went straight on, and the stranger lurched away after him, beyond the warehouses at the head of the pier, through the cluster of scattering native huts, and then up the slope of the hill toward the main town of Tupia, the white man's town.

Instead of keeping to the main road, however, the boy turned aside presently into a path that wound through scattering brush. It did not seem possible that this was a short-cut, but a South Sea Island brain knows more about terrain than any white man, and so the man from Kandava followed on with the black of shadows and the blazing white of the

64

moon alternately pouring over his face.

Above him, from the head of the hill, he could hear singing, and the throb of music that kept time for a dance. The man from Kandava began to sing the words of the song under his breath, when one of the shadows slithered out with snaky softness behind him. He caught his breath short and turned with a swing of his club, to strike with both hands. All that he saw was a shooting length of arm and a big fist; then he was knocked headlong.

Perique called: "All right, Liho."

The boy looked at the man on the ground and said carelessly: "Have you killed him?"

"Only dazzled his eyes a little," answered Perique. "Sit down on him, Liho, and keep your knife at his throat, when he wakes up."

For his own part, Perique had made only a brief examination of the man from Kandava, and now he had piled on the ground a big jackknife, a wallet with a little money and a letter inside it, a silver watch, two or three colored handkerchiefs, a plug of chewing tobacco, some matches, and a few other odds and ends.

Perique took the letter, opened it, and found the writing inside so heavily inscribed that he could read it easily by the moonlight. It was addressed to the captain of constabulary at Tupia, and it ran:

My Dear Wilshire:

As soon as I got your letter I made hurried inquiries because I wanted to find out what I could before the *Flying Spray* steamed out, today. I presently ran across Mr. Benedict Lawson, who will carry this letter to you.

Mr. Lawson seemed highly excited when he heard your description of the man called James Parry. He repeated several times, "Parry, Parry, Parry? . . . He's no Parry at all, if I have my guess right! I think I know who he is!"

I asked Lawson who he had in mind, but he said that if his guess was right he could give the captain of constabulary at Tupia news that would make his hair stand on end. He did not want to talk of it to any other person.

His exact words at this point were, "You don't want to start a fire unless you're ready to help stamp it out!"

He seemed in such a high degree of excitement, and was so determined against giving his information to anyone other than yourself, that I finally decided to let him have his way. I've equipped him with a round-trip ticket to Tupia and he will present this letter to you in person.

I rather think that he is not pretending and that he will be able to identify your strange adventurer.

I agree with you that if we can check the loosely wandering vagabonds who ruin the South Seas, we will have done more than half our work of civilizing the islands. With kindest personal regards, I remain,

Sincerely yours,
Charles Wendell,
Commissioner of Kandava.

Perique, as he finished the reading of this letter, heard Lawson groan, and said casually, over his shoulder: "Blindfold the eyes of that fellow, Liho."

The brother of Konia instantly inverted the tail of Lawson's coat over his head and tied it securely in place. The hands of Lawson he bound behind his back.

Perique, in the meantime, had scratched a match and touched the flame to the letter.

By this time Lawson was sitting up; he made no struggle to free his hands. He merely said in fairly good Lanuan: "Will you loosen the cloth a bit, friends? I'm stifling for the lack of air."

Perique came close to Liho and whispered at his ear: "Can you walk him into the forest?"

"I can handle him like a child, now," said Liho.

"Keep the point of your knife at the small of his back," said Perique. "He's a dangerous man, Liho. I'd go along with you, but I've been away too long already from the place where I'm expected.

"Be very careful. If he even so much as stumbles, be ready to drive that knife into him. He's a bad fellow, Liho, and the death of him would not be a great miss for the world, but I don't want your hands dirty with blood like that. Can you take him all the way to your uncle out there in the hills?"

"I shall take him as safely as though he were a bird in my hand," said Liho. "Perique, this is the sort of work that I love to do! . . . If I could follow you for a year, I would be a man, and other men would look up to me! Shall I go?"

"Go on with him," said Perique, and stood by to watch.

Liho kicked his prisoner with the bare of his foot.

"Get up, mangy swine," said Liho. The blindfolded man lurched to his feet.

"Take the end of this string," said Liho. "Hold hard to it. If you lose it, you'll starve in the forest before you ever find a way out. Keep the string tight and I'll lead you through the woods to a good place. You are not going to have your throat cut unless you try to run away. And if you try that, I have a knife that will cut through you as though you were white pig-fat. Do you hear me?"

Benedict Lawson said, steadily enough: "I hear you, friend. What have I ever done in Lanua to make enemies of the people?"

"What have the fish done to anger the fish hawk?" answered Liho. "It is only because I chose to take you. Follow me, and look that you keep the string tight."

He stepped off. The string tautened, and Benedict Lawson went hastily on at the end of it, holding it behind his back with his tied hands, stumbling blindly to the irregularities of the path.

Perique laughed, soundlessly, and turned to go striding up the hill.

CHAPTER 12

When Perique, coming up through the lower gardens of the house of Matthew Coffee, told those who inquired that he had been watching from the lowest terrace the arrival of the *Flying Spray*, the lieutenant of the constabulary, riding hard, was rounding the backs of the last hills and coming down into view of the lighthouse on Nihoni Point.

It was an excellent situation for a lighthouse because the point projected far out into the sea. Ships approaching would lay their course just to the north of this westerly light and so find themselves in the true entrance to spacious Tupia Harbor. But the lieutenant, staring ahead at the lighthouse, saw not a single flash from it.

The report of the master of the *Flying Spray* was true, then, and the light was dead!

This was a matter of such importance that it would be reported to the Admiralty, and the Admiralty of England raises the devil and all with infractions of navigation rules, and with all carelessness in land services which affect shipping.

This matter of the lighthouse might bring on a sweeping investigation which would turn the government in Lanua topsy-turvy. Governor Irvine Glastonbury, for instance, might have his whole face turned as red as his nose.

The lieutenant reached the bottom of the slope. There was before him, since it was high tide, only a water and moonwashed series of slippery rocks leading toward the lighthouse hill.

There were no means at hand of tethering his horse, but

Lieutenant Lawrence Clifford was a young fellow of resources. He was one of those pale, rather chinless Englishmen who look like baby half-wits and really have the stuff of fine steel in them. Lawrence Clifford had been so whetted by a rambling life through the world that he now possessed a cutting edge.

He was probably the most capable man in Tupia, unless Trader Matthew Coffee could be excepted. He showed a dash of resource, now, by using the reins of the horse to make effective hobbles. Then he started to cross the causeway of scattered rocks, awash in the tide.

Halfway across, he missed his footing and slid into the water. He climbed out, sat on the top of a rock, pulled off boots and socks, and continued in his bare feet. So it was that he came at last to the lighthouse hill, and he climbed up the side of the rock with some difficulty.

At the top, the ground leveled off into a terrace surrounding the lighthouse itself. And when he gained this height, he paused, even before entering the place, to look back toward the harbor. The entrances were clearly visible under the moon, for there were two gates to Tupia Harbor. That is to say, there was the true and the false gate.

Just to the north of the lighthouse was the opening of the true channel, fenced in between the mainland and a narrow island. On the other side of the island, still farther to the north, appeared the second channel, which was available for the use of canoes and other shallow draft vessels, particularly at high tide; but at the base of the false channel there were reefs which had murdered more than one mistaken ship. Nothing of the harbor itself was in view, because the higher hills rose and cut off the view even of Tupia on its own eminence.

Lieutenant Clifford looked, for a moment, at the fringing of tall palm trees against the moonlit sky, and then he went into the lighthouse itself.

There was no difficulty about that. The door was not

locked. He stepped inside and smelled, at once, the odor of kerosene. He heard a scampering of rats, like the noise of wind rattling dry leaves. Then he lighted a match.

The first flare of it dazzled his eyes. Then it showed him gray-headed Tom Washburn sitting at his table and slouched forward over it, his head resting on his folded arms. The back of the skull had been beaten in by a blow.

The lieutenant, not in the least shaken, lifted the chimney from the lamp and touched the match to the wick, but the wick was charred and would not light. In fact, the lamp was empty.

With a second match he found and lighted a lantern that hung against the wall. The flame spread across the wick. He closed down the chimney with a squeak of the metal guards and let the light rise and steady before he looked carefully about him again.

Tom Washburn had been eating a meal when he was murdered. The rind of a breadfruit, a section of which had been roasted, had been more than half emptied; the nibbling mouths of the rats had almost finished the rest of it. They had almost ruined the loaf of bread from which the dead man had been eating, but for some reason they had not invaded a dish of fried pork. Two slices remained in the pan on the table, cemented to the bottom with gray grease. Coffee half filled the cup at the right hand of Washburn.

The lights were more important than the inquiry into the death of Washburn at this point.

The lieutenant climbed up into the lamp-loft with his lantern. The big burners in front of the reflectors were not empty, as though they had burned out. But neither were they full. They were, perhaps, a tenth consumed, and this was of importance, for if the lamps had been lighted as usual a little before sunset, then they had been extinguished after they had burned for only an hour or two.

This might help to explain the hour of the killing of Washburn and made almost certain the fact that he had been slain by a man who wished to extinguish the beacon.

For what purpose?

That might develop later. But it was certain that Washburn would fill the lamps to the brim when he cleaned and trimmed them every morning, or at some time during the day. If the lamps were not full, it meant that they had been lighted and then extinguished.

If those lights had been put out, did it not stand to reason that someone had wished disaster to fall upon the steamer *Flying Spray* when she made her expected call that night? And yet it was a little strange that the murderer should have trusted the extinction of the light to completely baffle or betray a ship equipped with a strong searchlight.

The lieutenant, in the meantime, had refilled and lighted the lamps.

Now he returned down the narrow winding of the stairs to the room below and the dead man.

When examining a crime, it is better to go over details one by one, he knew.

He made note of the single room which served as living room, bedroom and kitchen. It was of good size, with three windows opening upon it. A small stove for cookery stood in a corner with a twist of stovepipe disappearing above it through a hole in the wall.

There was a shelf of books, a pile of magazines and newspapers to rejoice the soul of a solitary man, fishing tackle, a shotgun and old-fashioned rifle, a few clothes hanging from pegs, a chest under the bed, a washstand in a corner, a cupboard where food supplies were kept.

There was nothing to call the eye in any direction, strongly.

Here something tickled the bare foot of the lieutenant. He looked down and saw a moving stream of darkness that flowed over his toes.

He had stepped into the path of a column of black ants.

The dark streak ran on across the well-scrubbed white of the wooden flooring to a leg of the table, and up it to the top.

Across the wooden top the ants reached a little tin measuring cup, climbed the side of it, and disappeared into the interior.

The lieutenant, peering inside, saw the ants spread black over the face of granulated sugar, perhaps put out to sweeten the coffee of the dead man. The cup had not been entirely dry when Washburn filled it.

The result was that along one side of the tin the sugar had been stuck close to the metal by the dissolving action of the water. The mark ran up to the very brim of the cup, a sure token that it had been full when Washburn placed it on the table. A good two inches of the sugar had been removed by the ants, a grain at a time!

To Lieutenant Clifford came a thought.

There is no use making too much haste when one wishes to get at the bottom of strange events.

With the point of a knife he marked the present level height of the sugar that remained in the cup. And then he sat down to wait, in the doorway of the lighthouse, watching the broad glow of the beacon above him, a globe of brilliance filled by myriads of little flying things.

There would not be very long to wait. If the ants worked as they had done since early in the night, they would not be long in emptying the cup. And ants will always work at the same rate of speed. The finding of such a treasure as a cupful of sugar will bring out every worker, to the last one, and they will form their procession, half going and half coming. Tireless, they will continue their plundering until the last of the loot has gone to enrich the nest.

The running of an hourglass, the lieutenant knew, would be no more exact a measure than the steady drain which the ants were putting on that supply of sugar.

So, later on, when he had finished his cigarette with perfect leisure and felt the cool trade wind in his face for an additional few moments, he went back inside, expecting to find that the cup would be almost empty. To his bewilderment, there was hardly an appreciable lessening of the sugar.

Perhaps his interruption of the trail had set back the work? No, the procession was as well-formed, as thick as ever; the sugar was still black with the eager bodies of the workers. The returning half of the column each carried a tiny speck of white.

And yet the depth of the sugar had been diminished by no more than a sixteenth or perhaps a twentieth of an inch!

Carefully, earnestly, the lieutenant repeated that calculation.

Then he went back to his post at the doorstep and stared hopelessly out over the sea again.

The thing was entirely wrong. The ants must have been working with a tenfold energy a long time before his coming.

Suppose there were three inches of sugar in the cup when Washburn was murdered; allow only a half hour before the tiny little black ants discovered their treasure and started mining operations; that meant that in the space of some four hours they had excavated two inches of sugar. This was not in accordance with his observation. And yet it must be so.

Suppose that Washburn had lighted the lamps just before six o'clock, as he must have done. They had burned, say, about an hour and a half before they were extinguished—and Washburn was a dead man when they were put out. That made the time of the murder about seven-thirty, or thereabouts.

There could hardly be an error in this calculation. But, according to this, the ants had been at work about four hours—it was now nearing midnight. They had been scooping out half an inch of that sugar for every hour—and yet now their work seemed almost to have come to a halt!

By the time the brain of the lieutenant was beginning to grow frantic with this problem, another half hour had slipped away.

Then he returned and stared gloomily into the cup.

The thing was unchanged. But not exactly. Beneath the

mark he had made an hour before, perhaps a tenth or a twelfth of an inch had been mined away by the insects. No more than that!

Out of the dark of his mind the explanation suddenly rushed upon the lieutenant. The thing became perfectly clear.

Instead of four hours, substitute four plus *twenty-four!*

At once the thing was clear!

The ants had not slowed their operations. They had been working from the first at exactly the same rate. They had been working for some twenty-four or twenty-eight hours, taking a mere twelfth part of an inch away every hour.

Tom Washburn had been killed the night before.

He had been sitting dead at his table for more than a day.

It was not at the *Flying Spray* that the blow had been aimed. What ship, then, had been the object of this foul stroke?

Lieutenant Lawrence Clifford began to smile.

He drew in a good, deep breath of satisfaction.

For he was a fellow who loved his work, and he saw much work for him in the future.

CHAPTER 13

The dawn slips up as fast as the darkness dips down, in the tropics. And Perique felt the green fluttering of the eyes of dawn, and then the open day was looking in upon him. He sat upon his bed, copiously dressed in perspiration and short trunks.

Konia, cross-legged on the floor, was pouring little bright, white beads from one hand into the other—half a dozen of them. She jumped up when she saw that the master was awake.

"What is that morning song, Konia?" asked Perique.

"There are many morning songs, lord," said Konia. "Also, the man has been taken safely to our uncle in the forest."

"Good," said Perique. "Will he be held there until I give the word?"

"He will be held, lord."

"Even suppose that you and your family should learn to hate me in the meantime, will he be held there?"

"He will be held, lord. Why do you speak of hate? Except for you, Liho would be as dead as the pig we butchered yesterday, and in my father's house there would be only a female child left; and that is a very weak comfort."

"Very well, Konia. Where did you get those pearls?"

"On the floor of the room, where you dropped them, lord!"

"I? Dropped them?"

Without touching his hand to the bed, big Perique rose to his knees and stepped out on the floor. Konia examined him with a shameless exactness and smiled her approval of those big limbs with intricate snakings of muscles sliding about under the skin.

"Ah . . . on the floor of my room?" said Perique.

"Yes, lord."

"Damn this business of calling me 'lord.' My name is Jim."

"Jeem," said the girl.

"Jim," said Perique.

"Jem," said the girl.

"Let it go at that," said Perique. "Can't you say 'Jim'?"

"Jem," said Konia. And corrected herself, "Jeem, lord."

"Jeem be damned," said Perique. "But let it go at that . . . Look around for some more of those pearls, will you?"

"There are no more on the floor."

"They might have slipped under an edge of the matting."

"No, lord . . . Jeem, I mean . . . there are no more. Not even the eye of a kite could find more than I have found."

"Pearls," said Perique thoughtfully.

He began to walk the floor.

"Shall I bring you food, Jeem?" asked the girl.

"Be still," said Perique.

She sat down on her heels, against the wall, and waited. Nothing about her moved except the slow drifting of her eyes as she watched Perique up and down the room.

"Pearls—" said Perique. "Pearls on the floor. . . ."

He went to the iron-barred window and leaned his hands on the sill, breathing the fresher air of the outdoors. His eyes traveled down the steepness of the gorge. A hundred feet of almost sheer rock. Even a spider would have hard work surmounting that obstacle. Across the gorge, hardly twenty yards off, was the wall of one side of the big house of Matthew Coffee. Two eye-like windows looked blankly back at Perique. He began to squint. His jaw thrust out.

"Konia!"

"Yes, lord."

"Run around outside the place and come under my window."

She was gone in a moment; and then, with his face pressed close to the bars, he watched the golden flash of her rounding the corner of Bill Smith's palisade. She stood panting under the window. But she could not part her lips without laughing, it seemed. So it was blended panting and laughter together.

"Yes, lord?" she inquired.

He kept on looking at her for a moment before he said: "Look there in the grass. If pearls have been raining inside the room, perhaps they've been raining outside, too."

"Yes, lord," said the girl.

She dropped to hands and knees and began to winnow the grass with her slender fingers.

"One!" she called presently.

"Ah!" said Perique, and stood up straight, staring at the house of the trader, across the valley.

"Two!" said the girl.

Perique said nothing; he continued his staring.

"Three," said Konia.

There was a silence.

"There are no more, Jeem," she reported.

"Good!" said he. "When you come back, bring a blow-gun along with you, will you? The smallest bore you can find."

She was back again in only a moment, smiling, offering him the blow-gun. Instead, he walked to the end of the room.

It was long and narrow. He stood a dozen paces from her.

"Take one of those pearls and see if you can hit me over the heart with that blow-gun, will you?" he asked.

She nodded, put a pearl between her lips, and the blow-gun to her mouth. He could see the happy, mischievous glimmer of her eyes. Her breath whistled softly through the reed, and something stung the throat of Perique sharply.

He touched the spot, and grinned. Konia was running to pick up the pearl from the matting where it had rolled. She was as graceful as a bird on the wing.

Perique continued to rub his throat, softly, thoughtfully, as the girl offered him the pearl again. He took it as though it were nothing.

"Get a watering can full of water, Konia," he directed.

When she returned, he was standing, covered with soap, in a washtub of corrugated iron.

"Stand on that chair," said Perique, "and pour a small stream out of the watering pot on the back of my neck."

She stood on the chair and poured.

"You were drinking very much last night," said Konia.

"I'm always drinking very much after the sun goes down," said Perique.

"Is that good?" she asked.

He pulled out the elastic band of his trunks to this side and that, letting the trickling of water spread unhampered over his body.

"It is not good," he replied. "Gin and whisky are eating out my heart and rotting my brain away. Sing to me, Konia."

"If I sang, other people would hear what is only for my

77

lord," said Konia. "Shall I bring another can of the water?"

"No," said he. "But take that one away."

Before she returned, he had dried himself and stepped into trousers. He rolled them up to the knee and sat in a canvas chair overlooking the sea. He took a cigarette, which she lighted for him.

"Take one yourself, Konia," said he.

"Well, if I smoke often," she answered, "my teeth will turn yellow and my fingers will not be clean. I will smoke only once a day."

"Humph!" said Perique. "Hold out your hand."

She obeyed. He dropped the nine pearls into the palm.

"What are they worth?" he asked.

"They are worth a hundred fat pigs—no, they are worth a hundred and ten," said Konia.

"They are yours," said he.

"No, Jeem."

"They are yours," he told her.

"Yes, lord," she said.

"They are a farewell present," said Perique.

"Lord!"

"They are a farewell present, Konia."

"Do you leave Lanua, Jeem? I, also, am a sailor. Look at me! I can steer a boat in a high wind. I often take the steering paddle in a storm. All the men know that I bring luck to a boat. Look at me, Jeem!"

He looked down at the ground instead, and tapped the ashes from his cigarette.

"When you go, I shall go with you," said Konia.

"I am not leaving you; you are leaving me," said Perique.

"I?"

He raised his head, glanced at her, yawned.

He stretched his great arms and drew in a comfortable breath.

"Konia," he said, "you are such a pretty girl that I thought I would not see the yellow in the skin. But I can't help it. I like to have clean hands. And if I touched you, I'd be afraid that some of the yellow would rub off on my fingers. I'd keep looking to see the smoke in your eyes . . . so go away."

"Yes, lord," said Konia.

She went to the edge of the terrace and paused there.

"I am going very soon," she apologized, "but my knees are weak. And my stomach is sick."

"I'm sorry, Konia. . . . Here . . . have a drink of that brandy."

"It would not wash away the color of my skin," said Konia.

"Wait a moment, Konia. . . ."

"Farewell, lord," she said, and moved slowly away from the edge of the terrace.

Perique stood up to watch her go. The ash of his cigarette turned crimson. The heat of the smoke scalded his mouth.

CHAPTER 14

There is an approved way of breaking the spirit of any white man. They put one under the thumb of a South Sea Islander and let the islander work his will.

That was what they did with Stephen Gregory. He had fainted, thereby practically confessing that he had murdered Jackie, the night watchman of the Coffee and Coffee warehouse, and also he must have murdered Captain Ellis, or at least he must have stood by when the safe fell and killed the captain of the *Nancy Lee*.

So they turned over Stephen Gregory to an islander and told him to treat the white man as he pleased, so long as he forced Gregory to confess. It was an act at which the law winked broadly.

The islander was Tommy Molehua. He had been in jail a few times. He was one of those brown fellows that deteriorate most rapidly under the white influence. Vaguely, in his soul, he knew that the gin of the white man was the poison of his soul, and therefore he hated all the whites.

The constabulary had picked him up blind drunk, and half-drunk, and silly drunk. He had been beaten, and kicked, and dropped into the jail to sober up. There were permanently sore places in his spirit to match the bruises of his body. And it was to Tomi, or Tommy, Molehua that they gave Coffee's secretary.

There was nothing in the hut except the matting on the floor and a broken paddle.

When they were alone, Stephen Gregory started to fight for more than life. He started to fight for his pride of race.

True, Stephen Gregory was even more undermined in health than the islander, but he had a dash of the true pride. When he charged Tommy Molehua, Tommy avoided the rush, got him around the throat with the crook of his arm, and almost choked him to death. Stephen Gregory, ready to die, wriggled and waited, and then played dead. He was almost strangled in actual fact when Tommy paused to wipe the sweat from his dripping face. Then Gregory kicked him in the stomach with his knee and got to his feet.

He was almost at the door of the hut before Tommy overtook him.

It would have made no difference if Gregory had got to that door, because two of the constabulary were waiting outside it, but Gregory knew nothing of that, and thought that he was fighting for honor, life, liberty.

He turned at the door with the shadow of Tommy upon him and hit out with the last remnant of what had once been a good straight left.

In English boxing, you hit straight with the left, and then you cross with the right. That is about all there is to the game. If you are a reckless and wily devil, now and then you throw in a straight *right;* and you even uppercut now and then. But that is hardly gentlemanly. As for the devilish wiles of the American, who tears out the vitals with short dagger strokes not six inches long, the Englishman knows nothing about them.

Big Stephen Gregory, in the pinch, hit out with the straight left and immediately followed with a right cross. To his amazement, the two blows worked. The first one plumped on the nose of Tommy and blinded the eyes of the Lanuan with tears. The right cross, following, cracked home on the chin of Tommy and set him staggering.

He staggered back so far that he put out a hand to save himself from falling, and that hand luckily fell upon the haft of the paddle, where it leaned against the wall.

Stephen Gregory followed in, with a taste of more than blood, a ghost of his former hearty youth in his veins. And as he charged, Tommy caught up the paddle and whacked the white man along the head. Stephen Gregory fell on his face.

When he wakened, his hands were tied. Tommy Molehua sat cross-legged on the floor not far away with a thin dribble of blood still running unregarded from his nose, collecting on the point of his chin, and dripping down on his lap. Tommy had found a rope-end and with it he was flicking the body of Gregory, casually.

Even with his hands tied, Gregory tried to keep on fighting. He got up and charged like a bull. Tommy Molehua waited and hit him down with the paddle at the right moment. He used only the flat of the paddle because he did not want to kill Gregory.

The killing would have ended the fun all too soon.

So he only battered and bruised and started Gregory bleeding in a dozen places.

At last Gregory was knocked out again. When he regained his senses, the fight was gone from him. Britisher though he was, he felt that he was beaten, and his soul surrendered.

At this time, when he roused, he found that in the hut was the dapper figure of the captain of constabulary, Wilshire, and with Wilshire was Lieutenant Lawrence Clifford.

Lawrence Clifford was saying: "A gang. That's the only way to explain it. If the two things go together—and God knows how they could. A gang is the only way to account for it. Poor old Tom Washburn was killed the night before last. The ants told me that story. We know that whatever he did, Gregory didn't leave Tupia two nights ago. We have a complete account of his movements that night. Suppose that he killed Jackie and robbed the safe last night, still he was not out at Nihoni Point two nights ago. There's another thing to think about. If he stole the pearls and the money from the safe, why weren't the pearls found on him?"

"Because, Clifford," said the captain, "he was afraid that they would be found on him."

"If the pearls would be found on him, what about the money that was still held inside its brown wrapper? Wasn't that even a surer means of identification?"

The captain stood up. He walked over to where big Stephen Gregory lay on the matting, the Lanuan still flicking him patiently with the rope-end.

"Gregory, are you awake?" asked the captain.

Stephen Gregory sat up. "Well?" he asked.

"Are you ready to confess how you killed Jackie?" said the captain.

"I didn't kill him," said Gregory.

The captain turned on his heel and said to his lieutenant: "You see, Clifford?"

The chinless lieutenant walked past his superior officer and dropped on one knee close to Gregory. In this manner his face was brought a mere matter of inches from that of Stephen Gregory.

"Gregory," he said, "I'm sorry for this mess you're in. Did you steal the money we found in your pocket?"

"No," said Gregory.

The lieutenant arose and threw up his hands.

And at this, taking it as a signal of permission for more

torment, Tommy Molehua struck Gregory twice across his battered raw face with the rope-end; heavy, stinging blows. The manhood passed away from Gregory. He crumpled up and began to sob.

The lieutenant, white and drawn of face, signaled Tommy to keep away and shouted again: "Did you steal that money?"

"Yes!" sobbed Gregory.

The lieutenant, stepping back, rubbed his hands together as though to get them clean.

"Gregory," he said, "let's have the entire story."

"I found Jackie dead on the ground," said Gregory.

"How did you happen to find him?"

"I'd seen the pearl," said Gregory. "It was as big as the moon. As big as the moon! I couldn't sleep. I couldn't even drink, for thinking of it. I started to take a stroll back toward the offices. . . ."

"To steal it?" asked the lieutenant.

"I don't know. I was thinking about it and I just went that way, and I stubbed my foot on Jackie's body. I went on, then, at a run. I thought that with the night watchman dead, somebody might have got at the pearl of the *Nancy Lee*. I got in . . ."

"With what keys?" asked the captain, breaking in.

"The door was open, of course," said Gregory. "There I saw Captain Ellis dead on the floor and the safe standing in the corner. . . ."

"You didn't pry the safe off his body? It already was standing up?" asked the lieutenant.

"Yes. With blood on one corner of it. The blood still was running. I saw all that. I looked through the pockets of Ellis to see if he had the pearl. It was gone. I looked into the safe, where it ought to be. It was gone. Then I opened the cash drawer and I took the big roll of money. I ran out and gave the alarm. . . ."

"And you didn't get rid of the money?" asked Lieutenant

83

Clifford.

"I tried to think of a place to put it. It seemed to me that the night would be full of eyes to see every move that I made. I never dreamed that anybody would have searched me. So I kept the money in my pockets."

"What made Matthew Coffee suspect that you had the stuff?"

"I don't know. He's a devil. He can guess anything. The minute he came into the office, the money began to burn my body. It began to burn its way out of my pocket."

"That's exactly what happened last night?"

"So help me, it is!" said Stephen Gregory, and began to weep again, suddenly, weakly.

"All right! All right!" said the lieutenant, with a fierce disgust.

"Well?" muttered the captain, leaning upon the judgment of his inferior in this crisis.

"Let me get rid of that Molehua?"

"Do as you please."

The lieutenant tossed to Molehua a coin.

"You've done a good job, Tommy," he said. "You've been a good boy."

Tommy laughed and showed all the white of his teeth and the neat pink of his mouth.

"If you tell a soul what's happened here tonight, we'll hang you up a tree and lead a trail of ants to you. Understand?"

Tommy kept on laughing, but his eyes rolled crazily to this side and to that.

"I know," he said.

"Then get out of here," said the lieutenant. And Tommy left.

"Now stand up," said Lawrence Clifford to Gregory. Gregory rose, assisted.

"Could you walk home?" said Lawrence Clifford.

"Yes. I could walk, sir," said Gregory.

84

"Go home, then. Tell everybody that we've found out you didn't steal the money. It was planted on you. You fell downhill—that is the way you came by all the bruises. Understand?"

The open eyes of Stephen Gregory swallowed that sudden new truth and began to live again.

"Do I have my chance to kill Tommy Molehua?" he asked naïvely.

"Maybe, later," grinned the lieutenant.

"I'll go home," murmured Stephen Gregory.

"Have not more than two drinks and then come back to the constabulary office," said the lieutenant.

Gregory left the office. The captain made to follow him.

"Where are you going, Captain Wilshire?" asked Clifford.

"To keep track of him. I never saw you make such a fool of yourself before, Clifford."

"He'll come to the office," said Clifford. "You can have my skin if he doesn't. Who had the damned idea of letting a dirty native like Tommy Molehua beat up Gregory?"

"Gregory deserved it," said the captain.

But he felt the stern eye of the lieutenant upon him, and he flushed.

"I don't see that we're any forwarder," said the captain.

"Gregory told the truth. He didn't steal the pearls," said the lieutenant.

"He could have been lying."

"There wasn't the courage in him to lie.

"The courage had been beaten out of him by that Lanuan dog of a Tommy Molehua. He told the truth."

"Are you growing a little too sure of yourself?" asked the captain, frowning.

"I'm seeing something—just around the corner," said Clifford, as they walked out onto the street.

And there they met Nancy Lee, with the trade wind pulling at and tipping her parasol so that the green lining of it flashed and let in the strong slant of the morning sun on her.

Clifford saluted her.

He said: "Nancy, did Gregory steal the pearls, and all that? Did Gregory kill Jackie?"

"Gregory?" said the girl. "There isn't that much gin in the world, Lawrence."

The lieutenant looked at his captain with a faint smile.

"Where should we search for the guilty man, Nancy?" he asked. "You've lived in Lanua longer than any of us, and you ought to know."

"Of course I know," she said.

"Well, tell us, won't you?"

"Go search the new man, James Parry. Search everything around him. And see what you see," she answered.

CHAPTER 15

Nancy Lee went down the hill to the native town. It wasn't a thing for most white women to have done, but Nancy Lee was different. She talked such good Lanuan that they always believed her to be more than half of their own blood. Besides, the sun had darkened her almost to their own golden coloring.

She went to the big house of Kohala and found that giant sitting cross-legged in the sun, his head fallen.

She said: "What's the matter, Kohala?"

He did not rise. He did not even lift his head.

"Konia is sick," he said. "There is a cold devil lying under her heart and sucking out the warmth of her blood."

This might have meant many things. Nancy Lee paused for an instant, blinking, and then she hurried into the house.

It was all dim. The matting at the door was drawn almost shut, so that only a dim finger of light entered the dome of darkness and threw out a very faint glow into the corners. Konia lay on her face with Liho sitting beside her, patting her shoulder.

He lifted his face toward the white girl. His own expression was one of dull, stricken wonder. He kept on patting the shoulder of his sister softly.

Nancy motioned him away and sat down in his place. She put her hand on the bare shoulder of the girl.

"What is it?" asked Nancy Lee.

"Go away," said Konia.

"I don't want to go away. I want to know why you are sick."

"I am sick as you never will be," said Konia.

"How is that?" asked Nancy.

"I have yellow poison in my skin," said Konia. "He sent me away like a dog. He sent me away because if he touches me he's afraid that the dirty yellow will rub off my skin."

Nancy Lee looked suddenly upward. But all that she saw was the shaggy underside of the palm-leaf thatch, snow white outside the hut, but dingy brown and dead-looking within. Her mind stopped and recoiled upon herself.

"Well," said Nancy, "tell me just how you feel."

"Do you love me, Nancy?" asked the girl.

"Yes," said Nancy Lee. "I've always loved you, Konia."

"Ah," said Konia, "do you know what it feels to fall off a tree and hit on your stomach?"

"No," said Nancy.

"Did you ever make a high dive and land flat on your stomach, then?"

"Yes."

"That is how I feel. Hollow, and sick, and flat. I am going to die!"

"Do you know something, Konia?"

"I know a great many things. I know that he is brave and great and strong, and my master."

"Ah?" said Nancy Lee. "What I think is that he's just a beachcomber."

Konia pushed herself suddenly up to a sitting posture.

And Nancy observed, with true alarm, that there was no sign of reddening of the eyes. Konia had not been weeping.

Pain made her seem much older. That was all.

You can kill an Islander with shame. Also, they can be killed with fear. And sorrow destroys them, also. They are like the great lush plants that grow in the South Seas, easily wounded, easily bleeding to death, as though nature took small account of such a prolific race.

Nancy began to grow afraid.

"When you speak like that, you are a foolish little girl, and I am an old, wise woman," said Konia.

"Why do you say that, Konia?"

"Because I have eyes, and I see a man and know him. I see *my* man and know that I belong to him. Do you think so little of him?"

"I don't think pleasantly of him."

"I thought it was because of you that he sent me away," said Konia.

"Did he tell you that?" asked Nancy, growing a little cold about the mouth.

"No, he did not tell me that, but if he did not want me, what other woman in Lanua would he have? You know them, and every one of them, compared with me, is like something dead and flat and dull; like the eyes of a dead fish compared with the eyes of a living one. All except Nancy Lee."

"You know, Konia," said the white girl, "it may be that he doesn't take interest in *any* women."

"Ah hai!" exclaimed Konia, astonished. "How could that be? He is a man, is he not?"

"But white men are not all like Lanuans. There are white men who even go away from everyone and live by themselves. Konia, you are shutting yourself up like a silly girl. You don't open your eyes to see that there are plenty of other men on Lanua bigger and stronger and more handsome than Perique."

"Hush!" said Konia, springing to her feet.

"There is no one to hear the name."

"But don't whisper it, even. . . . They tell stories about that name, some of the old men in Lanua."

"Well, Konia, you go out and find a splendid young fellow of your own race to fall in love with you, instead of this one."

"They don't seem splendid now," said Konia. "Before he came, I was like one rich, with big pearls filling both hands. Whenever I went out to walk, I could look where I pleased among the young men, and they all were mine. This one was too short, and that one perhaps was too lazy, and the other was not very brave, but they all were worth thinking about, and one day I would make a choice. That was how I was. Very rich in my mind! But now there is Perique. I know how he feels about the yellow in my skin. I would not have one of my own people since I have seen him."

"I don't agree with you, though."

"You never have seen him except in clothes."

"Have you seen him without, Konia?"

"Almost. When I poured a can of water down the back of his neck, this morning, I watched it run over his shoulders, like light, and all the muscles moved and stirred like fingers under the skin. I wish you could have seen him then."

"I wish I could," said Nancy Lee thoughtfully. She added, with a little haste: "How is he marked, Konia?"

"As a man should be. There is a small, round white spot at the base of his neck and another on his left arm, and two on his right leg between the knee and the hip, and another on the calf of the left leg. That is where bullets have whipped through his flesh. Across his breast there is a long, jerking scar, like the form of lightning when it springs down across the sky. That is where a knife reached for him and cut him, and where the scar swerves is where the edge of it glanced off the bone.

"On one side of his head, under the hair, my fingers have

89

felt a thickening of the scalp, as though a club had grazed there and almost smashed in the skull. And inside his left shoulder there is a scar two fingers wide, and another part of the scar is behind the shoulder. That is where a spear went through."

"Did he tell you about the wounds?" asked Nancy Lee.

"Does a true warrior speak to a woman about what he has done?" asked Konia. "No, but I had eyes to tell what the scars meant. Well, he is gone away from me," said Konia.

She slumped down on the matting. Liho uttered a faint cry and came running to her.

"I thought you were happy again, Konia!" he mourned over her. "Konia, don't sit down. Don't sit down to die. If you die, we never will be able to go fishing together. If you die, the worms will crawl into your pretty eyes, and the lips will rot away from your teeth!"

Konia kissed his hand and then looked down at it.

"Yes. I know," she said, and sighed.

Nancy Lee stood up.

"Don't go," said Liho, and held out an entreating hand toward her.

"I have to go away and think," said Nancy Lee sadly. "Afterwards, be sure that I'll come again, Liho. Konia, if you love me, try to smile again and be happy. We *will* find happiness for you again."

CHAPTER 16

When he was inside Tupia Bay, Perique sat on a thwart of the canoe and filled its small sail with wind that carried him rapidly toward the mouths of the harbor. There the tide was ebbing, near the turn, but since he had to go a bit counter to the wind, Perique peeled off jacket and shirt and kneeled half-naked in the bottom of the canoe.

He had taken down sail and mast. Now he drove the narrow little boat with rapid, powerful strokes of the double-bladed paddle and the light craft skimmed through the true mouth of the harbor and into the sea beyond.

Here the large Pacific ground swell picked up the boat and set it swaying, but Perique drove on with stronger swaying of the paddle than before. Continually the blue water was lipping the mother of pearl that decorated the prow with silver brightness, but never a drop got into the hull. So he paddled beyond the headlands into full view of Nihoni Point, where the lighthouse stood.

The glass of its upper windows flashed red, as though fires were burning there even in the full light of the sun. When he had made careful note, Perique turned as the tide turned and with it slipped back toward the bay.

But now he swung to the side of the true entrance until he was able to beach his canoe on the island which split the mouth of Tupia Bay into two channels.

Some strong brush grew close down by the beach. He picked up the boat and hid it under some of these bushes. Afterward he patted his revolver, looked up toward the hills above, and then commenced to climb.

He could have gone up that height straight, like a springing goat. Instead, he chose to meander like a weak-legged old man, swerving far to the left and then to the right, his eyes constantly on the ground. In this manner he reached a first, a second, and a third brow of rising land, stepping back from the slope, and here he paused, taking note that he was about on the level of the lighthouse on Nihoni Point, which was just visible outside the inner headland.

Perique, staring still at the ground, finally shrugged his shoulders and sat down like a native on his heels.

The sun scorched his head and burned his wide shoulders, sleeked over with strength, but he enjoyed the heat. He smoked a cigarette, and seemed to be dreaming out to sea, but after a time, he commenced to turn his glance again about him. Instead of searching the ground, he turned his attention to the bushes which grew among the rocks. Among these he searched swiftly, often stooping to glance at the under sides of the shrubs until he found what he wanted—a broad, torn fracture of a lower branch.

He examined this tear, sniffed at it like an animal that can trust scent rather than eyes, and finally nodded his head with satisfaction. After that, he continued, but in a little distance he was able to find more and more of those same fractures, or other places where a hatchet had shorn through the wood.

In every case, dead branches had been selected.

And here an entire plant had been shorn off at the ground. He dug to expose the root, and found that, as he expected, dead also.

At this point he gave up his examination of the shrubbery, turned back on the shoulder of the hill, and took a squatting posture again and again, always looking out to sea. Now and again he turned about to dig into the sandy places or to turn over some of the loose surface stones. And after a few moments he found what he wanted: a spot where the gray rocks had been soot-stained with fire, and fire-scalded. They had been covered by other large rocks carefully placed on top.

He weighted the rocks with his big hands, and nodded again to himself. Still not satisfied, he continued his search under that blazing sun for more than an hour, among the rocks, among the bushes, and gradually descending, he came to the beach by the water again.

A rock, among the ten thousands, lay on its side, moss- or lichen-covered on two sides, but not the third. He went to that big stone, lifted it by the point, and stood it up. A crab with sprawling legs crawled out and slipped into the water. And underneath the stone were revealed a number of slabs of tin, such as could be made by cutting off the tops and bottoms of five-gallon oil cans and then spreading out the sides.

Perique looked once, then lowered the stone into place

once more. He returned to his canoe, and paddled it this time not back through the true mouth of the harbor but through that other channel to the left of the island. Here he came to a sudden smoothing of the water, the blue of it fading to a yellow green. In that slack of the waves, where the tide was checked mysteriously, he halted the canoe and peered down through the water until, by degrees, the form, the reaching arms, the wide jaws of the reef were revealed to him, growing clearer and clearer as he stared.

Perique smiled. He took careful note, now, of landmarks on either side of the channel, and then paddled farther on.

When he was satisfied of the distance, he stripped off the remainder of his clothes and dropped overboard. His left hand remained hooked over the stern of the canoe, pulling it down so that as he hung at arm's length his face was well under the surface.

In this manner he was able to gaze much more deeply into the caverns of the reef. Gradually he made out the form; it seemed to live with the drifting of the wave shadows over and across it.

When he had made it out, he lifted his head above the water and cleared his lungs with fresh air.

To climb back into one of those one-man canoes is a difficult and delicate task, but Perique managed it with a single well-balanced sway of his body. He stood up, whipping the water from his skin with the hard edge of his palm and letting the wind and the burn of the sun dry him.

In the meantime, the tide was bearing him backward toward the sea. By the time he had finished dressing, he was already beyond the end of the island, and now he kneeled and began paddling in severe earnest, hugging the shore, using the shallows where the run of the current was masked by the projections of rocks. In this manner he came back into the bay of Tupia and slid the boat rapidly toward the distant beach.

Meanwhile the young lieutenant of constabulary, Lawrence Clifford, seated in the shadow of a rock on Nihoni Point, was putting away a strong pair of binoculars in their case. Afterward, Clifford went past the lighthouse, spoke a few words with the new keeper of the light, paused again at the side of the new grave of old Tom Washburn, and then went on down to the shore.

His two paddlers at once sent the little outrigger away; the sail filled, and in a short time they had beached on the point of the channel island. Just where the strength of the glasses had shown Perique landing, the outrigger was put ashore.

"Now, boys," said the lieutenant, "find the tracks—where they go. Here, you see, is where a man walked over the beach not long ago. The sand still is running into the holes his feet left on the beach. Follow that trail. Tell me where it goes. There's a good thing in it for you. A brand-new fishing spear for each of you if you can tell me where the trail goes!"

They ran ahead of him, bounding from place to place.

Their voices came ringing back to him in the sea-wind.

"Here he climbs right—here he goes left—he sits on his heels like a tired old man. . . ."

The language had been well studied by the lieutenant, but still it remained a dim thing to him, coming faintly, obscurely, on his understanding. He followed in haste. They were running about him, like hunting dogs coursing over a countryside on either side of a hunter and his gun.

The gun of the lieutenant was the suspicion which he carried with him, at full cock. But he panted with the effort of climbing straight up the slope while those two active devils ranged here and there and everywhere on the trail.

When it was lost by one, it was recovered by another.

"Here he goes among the bushes. Here he sits down on his heels again and looks at a broken branch. Here he goes on again. Here he lifts a stone and puts it back to cover the fire-stains."

The lieutenant ran to the place and stooped to examine it. It was of surpassing interest to him. No native of Lanua would come by night to an enchanted island, a place of ghosts like this. The fishermen might land perforce on the shores during the day, but what one of them would climb this far up the hill and build a fire to cook fish?

So the lieutenant sighed and took breath. Whoever had built this fire was at least not a Lanuan, probably a white man.

For a place haunted in the eyes of a Lanuan would be haunted in the eyes of every other South Sea Islander, all so punctilious in the keeping of every taboo.

A white man, then, must have lighted that fire.

There was the trail now leading toward the sea, and the lieutenant followed the cry of his two hunters onto the beach where, presently, one of them was shouting: "Here he leaned and lifted and drove his feet far down into the sand. He lifted like this, and the rock arose. . . ."

The lieutenant, stooping, saw the flash of broad, bright eyes, and then made out the sheets of tin. For a moment he stared, and then with an exclamation he stood up and let the rock be dropped back into place.

It was very strange. And yet already his brain was fumbling at a meager thread of explanation.

They were in the outrigger quickly, again, and sweeping with the run of the tide down the false channel to Tupia Bay, the lieutenant marking the fall of the land on his right carefully, and sighting back over his shoulder toward the lighthouse to find exactly that spot at which he had seen the other stop his one-man canoe and drop naked into the water.

When that point was reached, the lieutenant had the two paddlers back water, while he stripped off his clothes. He showed a scrawny body rimmed with leather brown at the neck and the hands.

The Lanuans, when they looked at the naked lieutenant, merely opened their eyes a little wider. That is the Lanuan way of smiling most broadly. There is a greater mirth in such a look than in loud laughter. Each stared at the other and enjoyed the other's silent delight.

But here the lieutenant boldly dropped over the side, holding to the edge of the outrigger log with one hand, and so opening his eyes in the salt water until he was able to look into the depths. He had to pull himself up twice and gasp in fresh breath. But with the third descent, he made out a shape that wavered into definite form by degrees, like a thought forming in a struggling brain.

After that, he was helped back into the canoe.

He said: "Which of you is the better diver? Which of you can stay down the longest and has the best eyes under water?"

"I! I!" they shouted in a single voice.

"You both can go," said the lieutenant. "There will be not only a fishing spear but a bright new rifle for each of you, for this day's work!"

CHAPTER 17

"What'll you have?" asked Bill Smith.

Perique said: "Rum is to gin as woman is to song."

Bill Smith put back his head so far that the double chins turned into part of the full flow of his throat.

"That's a good one," he said. "I remember a girl down in New Caledonia—"

"Leave her in New Caledonia, Bill," said Perique.

"All right. All right. Only, I was just going to tell you something. How will you have that rum, Mr. Parry?"

"I'll have it quick," said Perique.

"You mean, nothing in it? Not even a squeeze of lemon?"

"I'm too damned sad for lemon juice," said Perique. "What do you do for a bad wound? You burn it out, don't you? And I want to burn myself out, Bill. I've got a suffering soul that needs to be purified with straight rum."

"What for are you sad?" asked Bill Smith. "You haven't even got rheumatism. Your eyes are good. You can eat fit for three men. And you got as long a life ahead of you as you want to take. What for should you be sad?"

"I've been thinking instead of drinking," said Perique. "What's that kava song?"

"I don't know. I've heard it a lot of times, but I don't know it. Do you?"

"Here's in your eye, Bill."

"Good luck to you, sir."

"Bill, that gin would be better for you straight. The stuff you mix with it no Dutchman ever had in mind when he made the gin."

"There's a lot of the world that lies outside of Holland, Mr. Parry."

"But God bless Dutch gin and Jamaica rum, I say."

"So say we all of us. Would you sing me that kava song, Mr. Parry?"

"I'll have another rum, first."

"Holy smoke, Mr. Parry, do you always take three fingers at a shot?"

"There's a reason for everything, and there's a reason for three fingers," said Perique. "The first finger is to sweeten your mouth; the second finger fills your throat; and the third finger of rum is what gets into the brain. The third finger, Bill, is what you might call the soul of a drink."

"Or the spirt of it, eh?" asked Bill.

A boy came running up, and bent to whisper in the ear of Perique.

"Miss Nancy Lee asks for Mr. Parry."

"Tell Nancy Lee to come in," said Perique. "I'm too busy to get up and go to her."

"Hey, wait!" said Bill Smith. "No woman will come in here except there's her husband or father with her."

"Nancy's father's dead, and she's out of luck about a husband," said Perique. "So I suppose I can't see her. Tell her

I'm too busy to come out, but I'd be glad to see her here."

The boy looked at Bill Smith, who expanded both of his fat hands in a gesture of surrender.

And so the lad went away, skulking a little, as though a weight were on his own conscience.

"Nobody else in Tupia would treat Nancy Lee like that, sir," said Bill Smith.

"Hey! Hey! She's coming!" he whispered later, as the messenger came flashing back to them again.

Nancy Lee came straight up onto the terrace there at the end of Bill Smith's place, walking leisurely over the green, keeping in the cool of her parasol's shadow.

"I'll see her alone, Bill," said Perique.

He stood up by the table. He had on trousers and sandals, only. Bill Smith moved away with a guilty look. But Nancy Lee came up to Perique and looked him calmly in the eye.

"You don't know that this is not a place for women to come, do you, Mr. Parry?" she asked.

"Call me Perique and make yourself at home," he told her. "I know that girls don't come visiting here very often.

"But Nancy Lees are different, aren't they? Will you have something to drink?"

"Nothing, thank you."

"Sit down and try the view, then," said Perique.

"I'll talk standing," she told him. "I've come about Konia."

"How is she?" asked Perique.

"Sick," said Nancy Lee. "Lovesick, and that means deathly ill for a Lanuan. If you won't send for her, she'll die for you, Perique."

"We'll keep that from happening," he answered.

"I'm going to give you a last chance," said Nancy Lee.

"How are you able to give chances?" he asked.

"A chance to slip away from Lanua. You can take Konia along with you. I thought I wanted to see you hanged for

98

murder; but not after I've seen Konia mourning. And then there's a sort of manly devil mixed into your nature, in some way. I'll tell you that your free time in Tupia is almost ended. Captain Wilshire has sent for Kamakau, Perique!"

"What of it?" asked Perique.

"He's the Kandava chief that picked you and Ellis out of the sea, you said, and put you down on the shore of Lanua without coming into the bay."

"What's wrong with that story?" asked Perique.

"Except that it isn't true, it's a fairly good story, I suppose," she replied.

"How did I get to Lanua?" he asked.

"The devil sent you here riding on a cloud, perhaps," said Nancy Lee. "I'm telling you that they're expecting Kamakau to come sailing in with his big outrigger under the full of the moon, tonight. When he's examined and declares that he didn't bring you in from the sea, what will the constabulary begin to think of you?"

"They begin to think a good deal already, I'm afraid," said Perique. "And so . . . shall I take you home?"

"I can take myself . . . You won't listen to me? Do you think you're not in danger, after all?"

"There's no fun in playing tag unless there's a danger of being 'it,' " said Perique. "I'll put on a shirt and go along with you."

She watched him pull a white shirt over his head. Even that slight effort made the muscles spring to life. They stood out in long tentacles, crawling under the skin of his arms and shoulders; they leaped out in quivering masses that flowed from the waist, widening upward toward the shoulders. A strange mixture of terror and disgust and admiration appeared in the eyes of Nancy as she watched.

She said, "You'd better not come with me."

"Why not?" asked Perique.

"The people in Tupia know I think you killed my father."

"And besides, I'm drunk . . . is that it?"

"You're not drunk. You've only thickened your tongue a little."

"Nancy, this Konia girl really has touched your heart, eh? You're fond enough of her to give the devil a second chance for his neck?"

"That's the answer."

"You're too noble . . . About Kamakau . . . that's nothing. He'll be glad to repeat what I've said. I'm not going to cut and run from Tupia. Not even for pretty little Konia."

She looked at him for a certain moment with more coming into her eyes than anyone ever had seen there before.

"What a brutal ruffian you are!" she said, and turned briskly away.

Perique laughed, reached for the rum bottle, and slumped down into his chair again.

He had not emptied a glass before Captain Wilshire of the constabulary and three of his armed officers appeared on the terrace, marching toward him with grim faces.

CHAPTER 18

The captain was in a stern mood. He said: "Hendricks, watch this man Parry. The rest of you come with me."

And he walked straight on into the long, cool room of Perique.

Perique said: "The strong hand, captain, eh? Searching without a search-warrant?"

The captain turned, glared at him, and disappeared through the door. Perique began to laugh.

He said: "Sit down, Hendricks. I'm not going to fly away."

Hendricks wiped his red, sweating face on the heel of his palm and answered: "I don't come inside of hand-reach of you, Mr. Parry. If you got any funny ideas in your head

100

about tricking me, I got to remind you that there's six shots inside of this gun and I was raised not to waste good ammunition."

"Spoken like a good Britisher," said Perique.

"It's the kind of talk that a Yankee can understand," said Hendricks.

"What are they searching for in my room?" asked Perique.

"Chicken feed. I dunno what," said Hendricks.

Perique lighted a cigarette, leaned back in his chair, and sipped the rum.

"A blue sea, and a clear sky, and a cool wind, and a lot of sticky hot British constabularies—that's what I need to make a good day of it," he said, when Captain Wilshire appeared with a gloomy face, his two men trooping behind him.

"Find the papers, brother?" asked Perique.

The captain said: "We'll have to stay here for a time. Lieutenant Clifford is coming up the hill to see you, Parry, and we may as well hold you for him."

"Sorry I haven't more chairs," said Perique. "But sit down on the grass. It won't stain your whites—not very much."

"You think you're the cat with the cream," said the captain angrily, "but I think you're going to have trouble, Parry. Big trouble and lots of it. Here's Lieutenant Clifford now."

The lieutenant came up the terrace looking pale rather than red. The climate was not suitable to him; it stole the strength out of his heart, his humid warmth plus any physical exertion. But his eyes were as bright as polished steel.

He gave Perique a short salute. Then he rested a hand on the edge of the table and said: "Mr. Parry, you went out in a small boat today. Where did you go?"

"Across the bay," said Perique.

"Did you land?"

"I went ashore for a few minutes on the other side."

"What made you go ashore?"

"Being tired of the sea, lieutenant."

101

"At what place did you beach the boat?"

"I don't remember. Where there was some white sand."

"That doesn't answer."

"I'm sorry."

"Did you go outside the bay?"

Perique looked at him for half a second.

"What are you driving at, Clifford?" he asked.

"You landed on the point of the island," said Clifford.

"That's true."

"After you got ashore, what were you doing?"

Again Perique narrowed his eyes a little. "I was following an old trail that I found on the beach," he said.

"An old trail? What old trail?"

"The sort of a trail that feet leave."

"Will you answer me frankly?"

"I'll answer you."

"Where did the trail lead?" asked the lieutenant.

"Up the hill on a zigzag," said Perique.

"Why should you have followed it?"

"I don't know. Curious to see whether or not I still had an eye for sign."

"Ah?" said the lieutenant. "After zigzagging, what did you come to?"

"Nothing important."

"Not some smoke and firestains on rock, covered by other rocks?"

"Now that you mention it, I believe I did."

"Afterwards you went where?"

"Down to the shore." Once more the eye of Perique glittered as he studied the lieutenant. "I followed the old trail some more. The footprints were quite dim . . ."

"Yes. I believe you. Quite dim," murmured the lieutenant.

"And so back into my boat and I paddled with the run of the tide up the mouth of the left-hand channel towards Tupia Bay."

"Did you go on through?"

"I remembered what I'd heard about reefs in the shallows. When I saw the water turn green, I decided to take a look at the reef. So I slipped into the water and took the look. The reef looked as dangerous as a shark. I decided not to take any possible chances—the least touch of a rock would have split my little canoe open from end to end—and so I turned about and rounded the island and came back through the main channel."

"What the devil is all this about, Clifford?" asked the captain.

Clifford did not even answer, so intent was he on ferreting away at the secret of Perique.

"You went down to the beach from the spoked rocks, and on the beach you lifted another large and heavy stone, Mr. Parry," said the lieutenant.

"I did. But there was nothing under it except some old tin."

"And that had no meaning to you?"

"Why should it? There's plenty of tin on all the beaches of the Islands in this century."

"Shall I tell you what that tin had been used for?" asked Clifford.

"Go ahead."

"Parry, there's no use trying to hold out. I have a complete case against you. A perfect case!"

"Go ahead with it," said Perique. "I like the way you talk."

"I'll begin with one other bit of evidence that will amuse you—and you, Captain Wilshire. At that place where Parry stopped his canoe and slipped into the water for a look at the reef, he wanted to see—and in fact he *did* see—far down in the water, the hull of a ship with its bow smashed in. . . . The ship is the wreck of the *Nancy Lee!*"

"Ha . . . Clifford!" cried the captain.

"I had my boys dive down to the wreck," said the lieutenant. "One of 'em got a life-belt off the rail and brought it to the surface. Nancy Lee was written on the belt."

"But the *Nancy Lee* sank far out . . ." began the captain.

"Exactly," said the lieutenant. "The *Nancy Lee* had to sink far out to sea. It had to sink out there, and not through a devilish bit of plotting in the throat of the left channel, the north channel to Tupia Bay."

Excitement almost mastered the lieutenant. Perique pushed a chair toward him.

"Sit down, Clifford," he suggested. "You're full of shakes in a way that I'm sorry to see."

"I'll keep my feet under me," said Clifford. "Captain Wilshire, we ought to have this man in irons."

"I'll do it in a minute," said Wilshire, "if you can tell me what charge to put against him."

"Murder!" said the lieutenant. "Mass murder. One of the most horrible crimes that was ever committed. An entire ship's crew wiped out, in fact!"

"Give me one scrap of evidence," said the captain, "and I'll load him down with a hundredweight of tool-proof steel."

"Good," said Perique. "Now the evidence, Clifford. We want facts. The British lion can't be fed on fairy tales. Facts, lieutenant."

Clifford pointed a sudden finger at him. "How do you happen to have pearls to throw around by the handful?" he demanded.

"I didn't throw 'em around. I wanted to get rid of 'em," said Perique.

"Ah, you wanted to get rid of them?"

"They came from Ellis," said Perique.

"Go on," said the lieutenant.

"Ellis was one of the first people I met on Lanua, after I landed and reached the town. After I'd met him and we'd had a drink together, I happened to tell him that I'd been landed by the chief from Kandava. He asked me if I'd do him a favor. I told him that my favors always brought a pretty good price. He put a hand into a pocket and brought it out with a dozen or so little pearls in the hollow of his palm.

"I watched the light wallow around among 'em. Ellis told me that he wanted to have his appearance in Lanua explained. He wanted it explained by saying that old Kamakua had picked him up out of the sea from a bit of wreckage. Ellis gave me the pearls and I promised to back his story and keep my mouth shut."

"And then you wanted to get rid of the pearls later on?" asked the lieutenant sharply.

"Yes, I did. The pearls had come from Ellis. Ellis is found dead. Naturally I didn't want the pearls found on me. So I gave them all to Konia."

"What about it, Clifford?" asked the captain. "Does that story sound straight, to you?"

"It *sounds* straight," said the lieutenant.

"It *is* straight," said Perique.

Clifford laughed, his voice squeaking up high and small. He was too tired. Excitement burned him up.

"I'll tell you exactly what happened," said Clifford. "And then you'll put this man in irons, captain."

"Glad to, as I said before," remarked the captain.

"I'll go back to the beginning," said the lieutenant.

"Once upon a time," suggested Perique, folding his hands behind his head. He closed his eyes, and drew in a great breath, then folded his arms across his chest and began to stare at Clifford with unfathomable eyes.

CHAPTER 19

"Murder breeds and grows fast in lazy weather," said the lieutenant. "We hark back to a time when Ellis and James Parry met on some beach. The *Nancy Lee* was about to sail

105

home. There were reasons why it should not be allowed to reach her port. All of these reasons don't appear. But there were plenty of good ones. For one thing, as Matthew Coffee has testified, there was a big pearl catch; a rich one. And the brain of Ellis hatched the idea.

"He would delay the sailing of the *Nancy Lee*. In the meantime, his partner in the intended crime—this fellow Parry—would hire passage on another boat, a native craft perhaps—that would be able to drop him by boat on the outer edge of Lanua without making the harbor at all."

"A boat from Kandava, for instance?" said the captain.

"A boat from Kandava, for instance," agreed the lieutenant. "But not one that landed him on the shore of Lanua when he says. Not at all. He had certain preparations to make before the *Nancy Lee* made harbor, here. As soon as he was on shore, he started to make them. They were simple, and surprising. He and Ellis were going to smash the *Nancy Lee* on the rocks of the north channel."

"How could they manage that?" asked the captain. "The lighthouse was out there marking Nihoni Point . . ."

"Suppose that the light on Nihoni Point was dark?" asked Clifford. "Suppose that the murderer of the ship first murdered poor old Tom Washburn and put out the lamps of the lighthouse?"

"Ah?" said the captain.

"Watch Parry's face!" exclaimed the lieutenant.

Perique poured rum into his glass until it was brimming. The liquor swelled up above the edge, held from running over the edge by the filmy strength of its molecular attraction. That glass Perique lifted to his lips with a slow hand, steady as iron. He drank off half the contents.

"To your story, lieutenant!" said Perique.

"His nerves seem steady enough," muttered Captain Wilshire.

"The man who murdered Tom Washburn and then

wrecked the *Nancy Lee* had to have good nerves," said the lieutenant. "Now mark how the thing happened. Washburn dead, the light out on Nihoni Point, and a ship running in under a dark sky towards Tupia Bay. Here's the devilish ingenuity—and yet the scheme was simple enough.

"He simply crossed in a small boat to the channel island and there, on a hill at a point about the same height as the lighthouse on the point, James Parry kindled a fire. To give the fire more brilliance and to make the light of it shine more steadily, he had arranged behind it some tin slabs that trebled the power of the fire and sheltered it from the wind at the same time.

"Now comes the poor *Nancy Lee,* sees the light, and takes the first open water to the north of it—the north channel, therefore, instead of the southern channel. The tide is running against her, but the trade is filling the sails. She bowls along at seven or eight knots. On board her, the sailors are a happy lot. Home is just ahead of them. And Captain Ellis is the happiest of all, because he has taken the cream of the pearl catch and hung it in a leather sack from his neck, under his coat.

"Then he slips over the side with a life preserver on and swims to the shore. In the meantime the poor little *Nancy Lee* is making full sail. There is a point of dark land ahead. When they round that, they expect to see the big, quiet width of Tupia Bay before them.

"Instead, there is a sudden line of white. What seemed only the song of the wind in the tophamper turns into a roar of the sea. They've rounded the point suddenly and the devil is reaching for them out of the channel. The run of the tide and the whip of the wind is tearing the sea to white pieces on the reefs. There's no time to do anything.

"That's how other ships have been lost in the north channel and never a man got ashore to tell the story. The same thing happens now. The lookout barely has time to yell out, and then the ship strikes. The teeth of that reef would disembowel even a twenty-thousand-ton ship in thirty seconds.

"The *Nancy Lee* is ripped to bits and goes down. Some of the crew make a hard fight for it to get ashore. They could master the wind and waves, perhaps—a few of the strongest swimmers—but the waves smash them against the upper edges of the rocks. They go down in one swarm. They die, every man of 'em, Parry, and you did that multiple murder like the cold-blooded, cruel devil that you are."

"You talk like a poet," said Perique, "but you'll never put the irons on me with such a yarn as that, my friend. Too circumstantial, lieutenant. Too damned circumstantial, I'm afraid."

"Captain Wilshire," exclaimed the lieutenant, "I've told you the story as it happened. Are you going to get the irons on Parry?"

The captain, his eyes hypnotically fixed on the face of Perique, said slowly: "Ellis comes ashore. He has the catch with him. The whole cream of the pearl fishing. He meets James Parry. He makes a split of part of the pearls with him. But not all. Some of the biggest ones have to be marketed with more care than they can use. So Ellis goes to Matthew Coffee and turns over half the prize, say."

"Exactly so," said the lieutenant, "and tells the cock-and-bull story about being picked up out of the sea. Matthew Coffee rewards him heavily, or is about to reward him for heroism, et cetera. But the reward is not quite what Ellis wants. Or, in addition, he wants a bigger share of the pearls. Crime is in the air.

"He decides to rob the safe. Remember that James Parry was on land to help. Together they go to the offices, kill poor half-breed Jackie, get into the office of Coffee and Coffee, and operate on the safe.

"First they decide to undo the wall bolts and roll or carry the safe away, where they can beat it open at leisure without making noise that will be overheard. But the job seems long. One of them believes that the keys of Coffee might be stolen. He goes up the hill to the house. And remember that Parry and Ellis were seen at one time or another at Coffee's party, that night."

"They were! They were!" said the captain eagerly.

"That thickens it up a bit," nodded Perique. "Go ahead, lieutenant."

"He returns with the keys. The safe is already free from the wall, but the keys are better. It's Ellis who tries them. Note that Parry stands by. He's discovered that the safe is easily overbalanced. As the safe door swings open, Parry gives the safe a tug. A hard one. It crashes down on Ellis . . . and that leaves Parry with the whole plunder in his hands. Do you see the scene, captain?"

The captain moistened his dry lips with the point of his tongue and nodded, still staring at Perique.

"Clifford," he said at last, "it's a beautiful story. It's the truth. I feel in my bones that Parry is the guilty man. But there's not a single iota of evidence to put before a judge. Not a scrap of evidence on which the law could hold him. Circumstantial, Clifford. Nothing but a chain of circumstances, and every one of them imagined, not seen!"

"But I saw him with my own eyes today, returning to the island and then pausing at the burial place of the ship. The criminal returning to the scene of his crime!"

"True," said the captain, "or simply an idle man taking a canoe trip out of the bay of Tupia."

"Captain Wilshire, think of what you're saying! You're not going to let that man go free, are you? After I've put the story of the entire crime on the table before him?" demanded the lieutenant.

"Give me a scruple, an iota, a single dot or dash of proof, and I'll have him in irons," said the captain. "Otherwise, for telling the whole story to his face, I will have to call you a very young man indeed! Or did you expect to break down his nerve? You might as well try to break steel with a wooden hammer."

Sweat was pouring down the white face of Clifford.

"The return to the island—going to the place where the rocks were fire-stained."

"It won't do. He says that he was following a trail. You haven't a dash of proof. He had a few small pearls. He gives them away to a girl. Find the rest of the loot and then I can believe you. Find a single crime ever lodged against him in the past and I'll hold him until we can try to work out this case. But as it is, Clifford, you've thrown away your brilliant work by the childish rashness with which you've used your tongue."

CHAPTER 20

It was after siesta hour in the house of Matthew Coffee. That afternoon some of the best people in Tupia were gathered there. The governor was among them. Nancy Lee was there. Captain Wilshire of the constabulary was on hand, and there were a dozen others. Matthew Coffee served tea in his "cooling-room."

It was an ingenious device carved into the solid rock of the bluff which supported the house and its wandering courts. One approached it down a winding stairs that passed two landings and so came out into that hall wrought out of the living rock. At one end, it opened on the hollow beyond the house of Coffee. At the other end, it opened on the gorge across which stood the establishment of Bill Smith.

There were many unique devices in this chamber, but chief among them was the cooling arrangement.

On the hilltop above, the trade winds blew without cessation day and night, through the year, and up there Matthew Coffee had erected two pairs of windmills. He did not need

110

them for pumping water, since a fountain already broke out on the ground in the middle of the court, but he used the broad-vaned wheels to operate circular sets of fans which worked beneath in order to drive powerful currents of air into the "cooling-room." These currents passed through rock-hewn tunnels into which constant streams of water descended as spray—the left-over water that ran down from the fountain in the court above. Freshened and chilled in this manner, the drafts of air were diverted by ventilators in any direction desired, and the temperature of the room was controlled perfectly. There was no period so hot that the "cooling-room" of Matthew Coffee was found too warm. In various ways the water could be used; one was to have a rain of it descend, or even solid sheets, that poured past the big windows at either end of the hall, so that one had a sense of life inside a waterfall, and the light was exquisitely tempered in the same manner.

In no way had Matthew Coffee shown more intelligence than in his skill in making all of these machines work in silence. There was only, at all times, a thin, small whining that sounded like the noise of a rising storm. But that was a small price to pay for so much comfort.

Matthew Coffee saw that his guests had an excellent high tea. The Honorable Irvine Glastonbury, governor of the island, turned his nose a shade pinker with a pair of tall whiskies, saying: "You understand things, Coffee. There's only one way to make a Scotch and soda. Fill the glass with ice, float the ice with whisky, and put in enough soda to crown the glass. You understand those things because you have a brain, Matthew. Eh, Wilshire? You have a brain, too, Wilshire. You'd appreciate a clever fellow like Coffee. What do you say?"

Wilshire said nothing. He merely smiled, and glanced at his lieutenant. But Lieutenant Clifford sat morosely in a corner, though Nancy Lee was doing her best to cheer him up. She had listened intently to the entire scheme of discoveries which Clifford had made and the heaps of evidence which he had accumulated against James Parry.

"There's no hope?" said Nancy. "It's certain that he's the man?"

"Why, Nancy, you've thought so from the first," said Clifford. "Except for you, I never would have dreamed of trailing him so closely!"

"I've thought so from the first," she admitted, "but still I had half a hope that I might be wrong. You know how it is. One can't help wishing that the thing might turn out better. I mean, he's such a big cut of man, it's hard to believe that he could be a cold-blooded murderer."

The lieutenant looked down at his own spindle-shanks.

"Size doesn't matter," he said. "It's the brain of the man that counts. But I'll manage to put James Parry in irons still! Yet there was the devil of it—that I should have laid the whole scheme before him. That I should have talked the whole thing out. I thought I would break him down with the weight of the evidence, but he kept his infernal, cool eye fixed on me, and was able to smile. Besides that, I was certain that I had enough in hand to justify holding him, at least. But Wilshire is a stickler for the form of the thing. He says that if there's so much as a whisper of real evidence against him, he'll put Parry in jail and keep him there until the case against him is complete. But he won't wait for the evidence. He'll be gone."

"I thought that the chief from Kandava was expected this evening. The moment he states that he did *not* bring Parry to Tupia, won't that be enough to put Parry in jail?"

"It will," agreed the lieutenant. "But suppose the fellow manages to slip away in the meantime. I've got to have him watched. I've got to have him watched more carefully if it takes the entire constabulary of Tupia to do the trick! I'm going to put three more men on the job this moment, as a matter of fact." And he jumped up to hurry out of the room.

It was almost at this moment that Matthew Coffee stood

up and squared his heavy shoulders and turned his big head slowly as he surveyed the people in the room.

"I think everybody here has an interest in my firm," he said. "I'm going to ask your attention while I talk business for a moment."

They gave him their attention with a sudden silence. His voice was calm, but there was a strain of nervous tension about him.

He said, still turning his head a little and looking from one face to the next: "Coffee and Coffee is bankrupt!"

Then he waited. The governor made a snorting sound.

"Five—damn—thousand—guineas!" he said. Then he swallowed the last of his second drink.

Coffee turned about and said: "Nancy, this is a frightful blow to you."

"Is it?" said Nancy Lee. "I'm not even thinking about it."

She went up to Matthew Coffee and put a hand on his arm, and smiled on him, her eyes moving slowly and thoughtfully over his face.

"If anything went wrong, it was in spite of you," she said. "*We* know what Matthew Coffee is."

He put a hand over hers, without smiling, and glanced back at the others.

The governor said: "I know—splendid integrity, personal letter of recommendation any time—but how? I mean, how the devil, Matthew?"

He waved to the bigness of the room. It was large as the hall of a palace. Through the showering, artificial rain the light came trembling through and shone along the beautiful patterns in the matting, and ran glistening over the great display of native weapons along the wall.

"You had the brain to do all this, Matthew," muttered the governor.

"Copra's gone to the devil. Coffee and Coffee went with it," said Matthew Coffee calmly.

"Yes, but don't be so damned noble and manly and all

that, and quiet about it," said the governor. "Tell us how
. . . and let me have another drink, Matthew, will you?"

Coffee waved to a servant who took the glass and filled it,
watching the signal hand of the governor in the meantime.

Coffee was saying: "Every one of you is hurt. Badly hurt.
I've given you an annual statement. It was always a good
statement. The point was that there was always a big item.
You remember what the biggest item always was?"

"Pearls on hand," said Nancy Lee.

"That's it," said Coffee. "Now they're not on hand."

"You are, though," said the governor, "and a fellow with
a brain like yours. Start again—start in a rock and grow
twenty feet in a year—damned wonderful, what a brainy
fellow can do."

Coffee faced the governor. "A man can't fail twice in the
South Seas," he said.

"Stuff!" said the governor. "Brainy man like you. Everybody knows you were robbed. All trust you again, damn it.
Absolutely all."

"Certainly, Coffee," said Hulbert Wilson, the first secretary.

But Coffee said: "I'm failing for twelve thousand pounds,
after twenty years of hard work, out here. There's not
enough soil for my kind of a plant. That's obvious. I'm going back to England and get to work. At the bottom of something. I don't want to be sentimental. But I have to say that
my life is consecrated to the making of twelve thousand
pounds as quickly as possible."

"Matthew, what was the value of the pearls in the safe?"
asked the governor.

"I hate to name the figure," said Coffee. "I'd rather have
my secretary do it. Gregory."

Big, red-faced Stephen Gregory, who had been making
himself invisible in a shadowy corner, stepped out into the
public eye.

He said: "There were pearls worth about forty-two thou-

114

sand pounds, Coffee."

The people in the room made, all together, a sighing sound.

"Forty-two thousand—"

"I mean to say," said Hulbert Wilson, speaking slowly and clearly, "that to keep such a huge stock on hand was rather a risk, wasn't it?"

"I'm not going to justify myself," said Coffee. "I'll simply state that the market was in bad shape. I've been waiting nearly three years to find the proper moment for selling. It meant something like a ten or fifteen per cent loss to get rid of them now. To sell at forty thousand or at fifty thousand. That was the problem."

He clasped his hands behind his back and waited, smiling a little, his chin well up.

Hulbert Wilson said: "I'm not striking you down, Matthew. I'd back you with everything I have. I simply asked the question. You don't mind, do you?"

"Of course I don't mind," said Coffee. "I have to point out, furthermore, that there never has been a penny lost from my safe before the other day."

"Ellis!" exclaimed the governor. "That Ellis—damn him—"

"He doesn't count," said Matthew Coffee. "Who was the man that was *with* Ellis? That's more to the point. Who was the murderer that struck down the old lighthouse keeper? . . . Who burned the false light on the channel island? Who sent the *Nancy Lee* jumping down the devil's throat? The same man—or the same gang of men—looted the safe that Ellis had opened. And whoever it is, is still in Tupia, I suppose."

Matthew Coffee raised both hands in a brief gesture. "It seems rather a pity that we can't locate the thief," he said. "It means twelve thousand pounds to you, my good friends. It means to me thirty thousand pounds in addition—and my sacred honor!"

115

He said the last words in a rather stilted fashion, emotion seeming to force out the syllable in spite of himself.

Afterward he said: "I shouldn't have put it that way . . . I think that's all we have to say to one another just now, though."

"There's one other thing," said Hulbert Wilson. "Wilshire and Clifford have been working hard on the thing. Is there any clue to follow, Wilshire?"

"We have plenty of clues," said the captain. "We know who committed the major crime. It's almost undoubted that he committed the second, also."

"Who?" cried the chorus.

"It's not law to spread a suspicion abroad until a man is found guilty," said Wilshire. "But I'm in need of help. From all of you. Unless we're careful, the man will spill through our hands and get away, loot and all. I'm going to appeal to every one of you to try to find out something, some vestige of criminal evidence on account of which we'll have an excuse to put in jail Mr. James Parry, that traveler from parts unknown! If we can jail him, I give you my word of honor that within two weeks we'll have enough evidence to hang him."

CHAPTER 21

A circle of Lanuan men were doing a masked dance for the benefit of the guests of Bill Smith. They had a central spot of fire around which they pranced. Some oldsters sat back on their heels and beat drums or rattled bones.

The picture was good. The masks were sufficiently horrible. And the guests of Bill Smith were highly entertained. When you entertain a guest, he will buy more expensive drinks, and more of them. Bill Smith knew that, but he turned his own back on the entertainment and came sweating up the terrace to the private ground where the hammock of Perique was swung between two palms.

Perique lay in the hammock with his eyes closed.

"Hey—are you asleep?" whispered Bill.

"Not asleep. Thinking, Bill. Has the sun gone down?"

"Ten minutes ago. They got trouble lined up for you, Mr. Parry. Doubled my guards with constabulary men. More of them watching at the gate. An' the whisper goes around that they're watching James Parry. Watching as though they wanted his head."

"Bill, that's too bad. I intend to take a little walk, this evening. Do I have to put that off?"

"Yes. You have to put it off."

"I'll walk down and enjoy the dancing, then," said Perique.

He opened his eyes and sat up.

"No, I can see it well enough from here," he said.

"You take it dead easy," said Bill Smith. "You know what they're doing? They're hookin' you up, some way, with the sinking of the *Nancy Lee*. What about that? What you think about that, Mr. Parry?"

"They don't know me, Bill," said Perique. "They don't know what a big, soft heart James Parry has. Get me a bottle of that bacardi, will you?"

"I can't, Mr. Parry. I keep that stuff in my own cellar. I can't send a boy to fetch it, and it means a fifteen-minute job for me."

"Go and get me a bottle of that bacardi," said Perique.

"All right," said Bill Smith. "Well, you got reason to want a drink, Mr. Parry. I hope you're gunna live to have a lot of 'em."

Bill Smith rolled his bulk slowly away. Perique, turning in the hammock, continued to watch the dancers, as they whirled and leaped. Then, half covering his mouth with his hand, he whistled a thin, birdlike note. He repeated it twice. It seemed to come from the upper air, it was so small and

117

unhuman.

At the second repetition, one of the dancers stepped back from the circle and sat down on his heels—something that all of them did from time to time. At the third whistle, the man faded from the firelight into the thicker darkness of the night and circled around the enclosure close to the high palisades.

Parry had gone back into his room, where he lighted a lamp, and the next moment there appeared at the doorway a huge, hideously masked figure. If the devil himself had appeared on the earth, he would have had to take to his heels at the sight of that tall form and that monstrous face.

"Enter, Kohala," said Perique.

He had thrown off his clothes, and he was rubbing a brown stain over his body, over his face, carefully rubbing it up to the lids of his eyes.

The Lanuan came slowly into the room, staring at the body of the white man.

"*Ah hai!*" said Kohala. "What teeth have chewed you, my father?"

"Little teeth that only broke the skin," said Perique.

"How did you know the call?" asked Kohala.

"I forget how. Konia told it to me, I think. Or Liho. Kohala, how is everyone in your house?"

"They live," said Kohala. He took off the monstrous mask and added: "But Konia will not live long. Her heart is sick. *You* have made it sick. However, if you save the life of my son and then take away the life of my daughter, I still owe you much. Women are not a great value."

"Konia is not like the rest," said Perique.

"No," said Kohala. "She has moonlight in her eyes. There is a brightness in her face, I think."

"I am going to take that sickness away from her," said Perique. "But the people are watching me, Kohala. If I leave this place, I must go in such a way that the eyes of the white man won't follow me. Have you any more of those masks?"

"There are three extra ones out by the fire," said Kohala. "Shall I bring one?"

"Keep it for yourself," said Perique. "And give me that one you now have with you. Also, give me half of that skirt of yours."

It was a thick brush of split reeds, made after the fashion of some of the skirts that the women of the islands wore in the old days. Layer after layer, it was built up so that it made a dense forest of growth and with the leaping of the dancers made a rushing noise, like the wind.

Kohala stared at Perique for a moment. Then, without a word, he took off four of the upper layers. Perique bound them about his waist and put the mask over his head.

"We've made two men out of one," he said. "Go back to the dance, Kohala. Has anyone seen you come here?"

"No," said Kohala, "unless they had eyes that could see in the dark. But how did you know that I was one of the dancers? Who told you?"

"The glint of the big scar, there on your right leg—that was what told me," said Perique.

Kohala laughed.

"Will you go to Konia?" he asked.

"Yes," said Perique.

"She will make such a song that the whole of Lanua will hear it," said Kohala.

"Have you a small outrigger that I could sail tonight?" asked Perique. "I want to go out a bit."

"It is too small for such a wind," said Kohala. "There is too much wind even in the bay, and the storm is coming."

"Have you such a boat?" asked Perique.

Kohala, struck very sober, stared again at the white man.

"*I* shall go with you, then," he said.

"You'll stay here," said Perique. "Stay here with the dance. You know, Kohala, when a man goes on a narrow path he must go alone."

"And how far do you go?"

"As far as my luck lets me," said Perique. "Farewell, Kohala."

Kohala, backing out of the room, faded slowly into the darkness. Afterward, Perique followed.

He drifted through the outer night toward the light of the little bonfire around which the dancers were now prancing wearily. The drummers vainly tried to freshen the music, for the Lanuans were spent by their work.

Perique sat down on his heels, watching the big, gleaming bodies for a moment. Then he rose and went on toward the gate of the place. He moved slowly. The heat of the night set him gleaming with perspiration. His lips parted with a noisy panting. And as he came to the brilliant light of the gateway, the two armed men who waited there gave back a little.

Perique walked slowly on down the street. He shifted the rustling skirt a little. It was binding him hard about the loins, because under its layers he had bound next to his skin a pair of white trousers and a linen shirt. There was hardly room for so much extra padding.

Bill Smith, returning with the bottle of bacardi, came up on the terrace singing, when he discovered that the hammock was empty.

"Hey, Mr. Parry!" he called.

He went to the door of the room. "Hey, Parry—" he began.

Then he saw the emptiness and was struck silent.

"Stole!" he breathed. "They've stole him!"

CHAPTER 22

Perique went on down to the native village at the bottom of the hill. He walked through the points and slashes of lamplight, and the dull, red flicker of firelight, but on the whole there was little illumination to see features by. The sharpest eyes in Lanua could not have told him from a native.

Overhead, the stars trembled and now and then they went out as clouds flew across the sky. A storm was coming up, as had been said by Kohala. Among the waves that beat on the beach, an occasional one struck with alarming force and spoke with a loud, booming voice, an alarm signal.

A wave of children came dashing down the "street" through which Perique was passing. The yelping of dogs raced along with the noise of the youngsters. Perique stood still, his eyes half-closed, and let that wave of noisy life rush past him as a surf bather might have stood for the wash of a breaker.

Then he laughed and went on to the house of Kohala. At the entrance, he paused, and heard the voice of young Liho singing.

Perique pushed the hanging away from the door and glanced in. Konia lay face down, her head obscured by the dark, flat pool of her hair, widely spreading. A little red and green rooster, as though mistaking the firelight for the sun, had roused himself from his roost and was picking at the matting not far from the girl. Liho, his face held between his hands, regarded his sister with a sullen despair.

Perique, lifting his head, found in his mind the proper thing to do. You can find songs of all sorts among the Lanuans, but the old love songs are the most numerous, and he began to sing, not loudly, but with that gong-like resonance breaking into his voice in spite of himself.

Konia, when she heard the first words, started to her knees, sweeping back her hair with both hands, and in the middle of that gesture she remained frozen to brown stone, staring at the tall figure in the doorway. Liho, when he had a first glance at the intruder, picked up a fishing spear with a long, dangerously barbed head. He held that spear poised for the cast, frowning angrily; but Perique leaned at the doorway

121

and sang the song through to the end.

"Perique!" said Kohala, and jumped to her feet.

He came striding in, the leafy skirt jouncing around his knees.

"Perique!" said Liho, and tossed the spear aside.

"Do you come for my father, lord?" said Konia, trembling.

"No, but I'm wearing part of his clothes," said Perique, taking off the hideous mask from his head.

"Do you come for Liho, lord?" said the girl.

Perique laughed, and for an answer he sang that song which, in the old days, was reserved for the lips of Lanuan princes and heroes only. It goes:

I have been very far away from you.
The high green mountains of twilight lay between us.
The terrible dark ocean of night lay between us.
I journeyed on through the storm, hopeless,
And suddenly I reached the white beach of the dawn,
I saw my home and the bright morning of your face.

Konia, listening, was trying to put back her hair in order, but her hands stopped against her will and forgot what they were doing. As he ended, Liho said: "I told you he would come for you or send for you, Konia."

"Say it, lord," said the girl.

"I've said enough. Singing is better than saying," said Perique. "Liho, I'm going for a sail. Will you show me your father's outrigger?"

"You would not sail outside the bay on such a night?" asked Liho.

Perique raised his head and listened, for the wind screamed suddenly at them and the roof of the house shivered.

"You must not sail even on the bay in such weather," said Liho. "But sit down with us, lord, and eat."

Before Perique could answer, the girl had said: "Liho,

122

when a man speaks, a boy should be silent. Go lead the way to the boat."

"*Ah hai,* Konia," said Liho, "now that he almost has said that he loves you, do you want the sea to eat him, bones and all?"

"The sea takes what the gods give it," said the girl. "Shall *I* show you the boat, lord?"

"Look at her!" said Liho, wondering. "Only five minutes ago she looked as pale and dead as the belly of a shark. And now it's as though the sun had been burning her all day long. How can you change so soon, Konia?"

"My lord knows," said Konia. "Shall we go?"

They left the house. The wind struck them, putting a heavy shoulder against their bodies, so that Liho staggered a little, but then laughed and went running ahead of them very happily.

When they got out on the beach, there were no stars to be seen on Tupia Bay. The waves came rapidly in shore, slapping the beach in an excited hurry. Thin drivings and gusts of spray stung the face and made the lips salty at once.

"*Ah hai!*" cried Liho. "Who would even want to go out on the bay in this sort of a night? It is dark! It is too dark! But not too dark for death to smell a man, like a shark. Lord, stay warm and safe with us on shore."

The girl waited for a moment, her face lifted toward Perique as she stared at him. Then she said: "His mind is fixed. When the mind of a man is fixed, the women and children should be silent, Liho. Here, lord, is the boat."

They ran it down the sand into the water. Liho lifted the log of the outrigger so that it would not cut into the beach and make the work harder. Perique and the girl handled the canoe. It was richly done with pearl about the sharp ends; there were still enough stars to make the ornaments glimmer dimly.

Now the craft slipped into the water. The rapid waves

began to knock the head of it around.

Liho and the girl stood shoulder-deep, steadying the outrigger.

"Ready!" called Perique.

He was hoisting the sail of heavy matting.

A voice called close to him: "I can tend the sail, lord. Let me come with you!"

"You are only a girl, Konia," he said.

"Even to die, lord, it is better to have company," she answered.

He, for reply, reached down a big hand, caught hers, and agile as a flying fish she slipped aboard.

"*Hai! Hai!* Let me come too!" shouted Liho.

But the wind now filled the sail and made the light little outrigger leap over the waves like a galloping horse. The arms of Liho gesticulated in the darkness for a moment; his voice screamed after them like a sea-bird's. And then he was gone.

CHAPTER 23

There were a pair of paddles under the cleats at the bottom of the craft. Perique used one of these for the steering, and Konia held the sheet, paying out or hauling in with the most expert craft, and so managing the matter that she often had the narrow log of the outrigger quite clear of the water, merely kissing the crests of the waves. When she managed this, the boat leaped with a new life. It seemed to outrun the quartering wind that drove it. And the impacts of the waves blurred rapidly together until it seemed that they were being exploded upward into the air by the number of those shocks.

So they leaped like a great, sleek fish across Tupia Bay and headed for the harbor channel. The land on either side of the narrow outlet began to run dark with speed through either corner of the eye of Perique. The wind was nearly aft, now, and the outrigger wallowed a little with the clumsy force of it, since all boats that sail, if they have manhood in them, love best a wind quartering, or abeam.

They slid out past the black sharknose of the island; they had before them the yellow gleam of the light on Nihoni Point, its rays scattered obscurely across the waters, here and there, wherever the light could find a spot of smoothness in which to be reflected.

Perique held on toward the light until he was clear, or almost clear, of the headland on his right. Then he shouted to Konia, and steered toward the north into the open sea. He could see the sudden turning of her head, and a faint gleam of light that seemed to issue from the sea showed a glint along her throat and arm. But afterward she pulled the sheet in until the mast groaned with the leaning weight of wind that filled the sail. Once more she had the outrigger log lifting from the waves. Once more they were skimming like a bird.

A savage wonder touched Perique. What other Lanuan, among the most daring of the sailors there, would have dared to venture out to the open sea in such a wind, among such waves?

Here they had cleared the shelter of the land, and the great ground swells of the Pacific, built up by five thousand miles of powerful trade winds, began to hump their backs under the little boat.

It was like climbing hills. In the trough, the wind failed them, the sail went slack, joggling aimlessly on the mast. And then as the shoulder of the next wave tossed them up, lightly, staggering into the wind, the sheet had to be played and steadied with the most expert hand, the steering paddle had to work desperately in the sway of water made hard with speed, so that the nose of the canoe might point true and the gale used like a friend.

The power of that wind, if it caught them wrong, would smash them down into the waves like a fierce hand.

The sword of the gale struck whistling past them. They had to use the edge of it—the tooth of it, as the old Lanuan song has it.

At that moment a yellow fire bloomed in the east, ran over the wilderness of the sea toward them. That was the rising moon, puffed larger by three times than her true size, now a shining ball flung up from the horizon, with the lift and spring of the waves darkening her face.

The skirts of a storm poured shadows across that moon and turned her face gray. But once more she was looking vaguely through the squall as it sprang on the little boat.

"Into it! Into it!" called Perique.

"Aye, into it!" cried the girl. "Split the wind like an ax. Split it down the smooth grain and we'll come through safely!"

He, with immense paddle strokes that set his shoulder cords straining and creaking like a mechanism of ropes and iron, swung the head of the canoe about; and as the dark feet of the storm ran upon them, the girl trimmed the sail in flat, so that it cut the wind like a knife.

On a powerful ship the thing can be done. What is the old rule? Never take in sail for a squall you can see through. Knife the sails with flat, straight edges through the gale and wait for the fury of the wind to die before you try to use it again.

In a big ship that can be done by a skillful helmsman and a swift crew; but the little outrigger with its sail of matting was like a toy made of paper. Only the sheer edge must be presented to the storm. If it veered the slightest bit from the hurricane, it would be struck flat, capsized, and then in a moment two lives would be cast into the waters, two human heads would be struck by the lurch and the beat of the combers until they went down for the last time.

Two lives like two grains of salt, they would be dissolved.

But as the wave heaved them up, they cut the wind truly, steadily. Then a black-backed monster of a wave swelled up and gave them a lee—a lee of danger, for they must feel their way up the rise and crazy crest-swing of the next roller and straight on into the wind again.

So the girl, glancing back, saw the moonlight gilding faintly the long, wind-streaked hollow flank of the wave.

And the water sucked into deep, sudden mouths of black about the laboring paddle of Perique.

The next moment she was working at the sheet with cunning hands as they came over the bulging forehead of the wave. The edge of the wind slid under the upward driving prow. It lifted, staggered the whole of the little craft—and then the paddle bent in the hands of Perique as the rapid strokes swung the head of the boat right into the wind. The sheet played in the wise hands of the girl. God praise the seamanship that was born into the generations of her blood!

Yet they were not through. The wind put down its hand flailings upon them. They wallowed deep. Spray seared their eyes and burned their faces; spray in choking blasts. The edges of the gunwales staggered down under the lip of the wave. Leaden heavy water poured in on them. And then the trough of the wave descended with them.

They were shooting downhill into the slack of the wind. They would shoot straight on, perhaps, into the heart of the next roller, and so to quick destruction.

The moon would see them. That was all. And back there in Tupia was the smell of roasted breadfruit, the humming voice of the far-off song, the babble of playing children among the thatched houses, now being silvered by this same moon.

Konia, as they slid down out of the wind, dropped the sheet, turned with a flat of cloth in her hands, and began to bail with all her might. Perique could not help her. His skill would be in guiding the canoe down the cataract of water, so aiming it that the nose might come a little askance on the opposite hill of the wave, and so perhaps glance up it. If only the bailing could lighten the depth of the canoe a little! Only a little, there toward the head!

He could see her clearly enough through the beat of the rain that had the moon behind it. The squall had grown shallower and shallower. It had almost blown over. The light of the moon was being strained through the skirts of the downpour to show Perique the frantic work of the girl. But fear had not distorted her face; she fought with the honest enthusiasm of one who does not doubt a victory!

And now they were on it—the last downward lurching run into the trough, aimed like a spearcast at the opposite wall of water.

He swerved the bows. They struck—they were buried in the sea.

No, they had indeed glanced. They were lifting. The water streamed away. The wave flung them up, up—into the unclouded light of the moon, and the squall rushed on past them with a roar and a screaming.

Konia, again at the sheet, payed it out slowly. The wind, no longer a terrible sword-stroke, was again their dangerous and gigantic servant to whisk them over the ocean.

"Down there to the leeward! The leeward! Do you see, Konia?" shouted Perique.

She pointed an arm that glittered with water and moonlight. She, also, had seen the sweep of the shadow across the face of the moon, like the flick of a bat's wings before a light. Some other boat, more powerful, was daring the way across the stormy ocean, making desperately for the shelter of Tupia Bay.

"We run for that!" called Perique. "The devil's in my spinal marrow. I can feel him gritting his teeth on my bones. This is my night for luck, Konia! Away for them!"

So swerving a little, with the wind quartering once more, they took the gale on the opposite side and began to sweep down toward that other craft.

It carried a light fore and aft. They could see it again and again, in flashes and broader glimpses, a monstrous, low-hung sail and beyond a powerful hull the lifting, the thrash and the plunge of the outrigger; taking punishment that would break iron, so it seemed.

For that goal they ran the canoe until the huge thamakau was right in their lee and dark figures of men stood up along the side of the big ship, clinging to the rigging as they stared at this little sea-bird which was winging its way toward them, this stormy petrel skimming the waves.

CHAPTER 24

So aimed that it would just miss the stern of the big thakam-bau, the little outrigger flew into the spray knocked up by the other ship. And at the proper moment a rope was flung like a filmy snake through the moonlight. Konia, alert in the bow, caught the rope and fastened it with a half hitch; the next moment the outrigger was twisted about onto its new course, with a jerk that almost buried it under the sea.

The two of them had to bail furiously to keep the boat from settling. But now they were reasonably safe as the tiny craft danced on the boiling wake of the ship, almost under the shadow of the great, reaching stern.

"Stay here and bail," said Perique. "But keep one hand on the rope. If the boat ducks under, I'll go after you, Konia, and stay under till I find you or a shark— Be careful—I won't be gone long."

She smiled and waved a hand. The wind had knocked her hair loose and she put it up in a knot. Water gushed out of it. She was wet from head to foot, and the moonlight gilded her as she stood there heedless, swaying to the bucking and caper-ing of the boat. She went back to the steering paddle, and

Perique ran up the big rope to the thakambau with the agility of a monkey.

Over the high reach of the stern, he swung himself into the narrow trough of the hull where two strong men were holding the ponderous steering paddle. Forward, the sides of the canoe were raised by planking which then was decked over. Fore and aft of the decking in the open wells stood men bailing with wooden scoops, keeping a constant stream of water going over the sides, for the planking, insecurely caulked, was sure to work enough to let in a good deal of sea in such heavy weather. To operate this huge canoe, a crowd of forty chosen men were on board. For it was a vessel belonging to a man of immense importance, Kamakau himself. England and France had stolen half his power away from him, but still he was a king.

And like a king he sat now, cross-legged, on a sort of raised dais on the deck. As the great canoe pitched and labored, he kept his place by holding onto a rope; and on either side of him crouched a wife from his large establishment of females on shore. Perique was instantly before him. Strong hands had helped him on his way, and in his ear was the name: "Perique!" constantly repeated.

The two wives of Kamakau made a shrill outcry when they saw him. The chief himself extended a hand as big and strong as that of Perique himself and drew him down onto the deck.

"What are you doing, brother, in such a small boat in such a big sea?" asked Kamakau. "*Ah hai!* Look at the thunder blackening its face there in the sky. The wind has been kicking water into my face for hours. Why are you out in this weather, Perique?"

"If an old friend comes," said Perique, "I always go outside my house to meet him."

Here the wind whistled a cloud of driving spray off the waves and sent it rattling on board, drenching everyone. But since all had been drenched a hundred times before, no one paid the least attention to this little calamity. For, however strong the wind might blow, it was warm. Before them the heights of Lanua's inland mountains loomed where the moon struck them and disappeared where the shadows of the storm lay.

Kamakau had the head of an old man and the body of a youth. He had a long wrapping of fine white cotton around his middle and no other clothes.

He was saying: "But now you bring a wife with you when you travel? You should have two, Perique. Every man should travel with two wives, as I do. One is for bad weather and one is reserved for good."

"That girl in the outrigger is not a wife," said Perique. "She is only a friend."

"*Ah hai!*" said Kamakau. "Can you teach your friends to follow you on such a sea as this? . . . Have you saved them all from guns and knives? Can they all remember, like Kamakau, just how death grins like a skull, and then Perique coming at the last moment?"

Here the wind knocked the big boat awry with a terrible shuddering. Perique sprang to his feet and saw the little canoe behind them still staggering. The arm of Konia flashed as she waved to him.

"Kamakau," said Perique, when he sat down again, "you are coming all the way to Lanua because the governor wants you, and the chief of the constabulary has sent a letter asking you to come here and tell him about a certain man in Tupia . . ."

"When the man of the constabulary writes, I always read," said Kamakau. "Reading is a bad work for me. It makes my head ache. Reading for one hour makes me want to be drunk for a day. But the constabulary carry fine new rifles. You have to pay attention to a man with a rifle."

"Of course you do," said Perique.

"Unless," said Kamakau, "you are like Perique, and can take the rifle away and break the stock of it over the fellow's head. But we are not all like you. We cannot wave bullets aside with our hands."

"That man in Tupia," said Perique, "is one who says that he was brought over the sea by you and landed on the outer beach of Lanua. That beach there—you can see the white of it just now. Now the shadow covers it again. The man says that you brought him all the way from Kandava in this same ship of yours."

"The man lies," said Kamakau, "and I shall tell the captain of the constabulary so."

"Does a friend ever lie?" asked Perique.

"No, I suppose not," said the chief.

"And am I your friend, Kamakau?"

"Ah—ah—is it you who said so?" demanded Kamakau.

"I said so."

"Then I remember the very day when I brought you."

"Thank you," said Perique.

"Will it mean much to you?"

"A rope around my neck, Kamakau."

"I remember," said the chief, "that when we were sending you ashore in the canoe, a breaker tumbled the boat aside and you jumped into the water and swam ashore."

"No," said Perique. "You remember that I was wearing a good suit of white cloth."

"Ah—true—true! I forget that you can be a white man also."

"So we made a dry landing. You came ashore with me."

"And barked my shin on the gunwale of the canoe. I can show them the mark."

"Good!" said Perique.

"What else can I do?"

"How long would you stay in Tupia Bay?"

"Only a week. Only long enough to be drunk twice on brandy and once on beer."

"Kamakau, all the men in your boat know me."

"I would beat them with my own hands if they did not

132

know Perique. *Ah hai,* there is not a house among my people that is not your house, Perique."

"But, Kamakau, when men drink, they talk with a bigger tongue. Here you have forty men, and if the constabulary starts asking questions when they are drunk, how long can they keep the secret? How long before they will be telling that James Parry is Perique?"

"True!" muttered Kamakau. "I see that I have business which will take me away again, at once. I shall not even let a single man go ashore."

"Kamakau, you are a friend."

"I should be dead, otherwise," said Kamakau cheerfully. "My windpipe still aches where the hands of that devil were gripping it. And I can still feel the hot of his blood when it gushed over me. And I remember how his head fell back—"

"Hush!" said Perique. "You'll frighten your wives!"

"Frighten them? They tell their children the story of Perique."

"Not all of it, I hope."

"No. Not the talk that fools make. Not the talk that comes from the other islands. Talk that comes out of the sea is only good for the fish; let them believe it."

Perique laughed. He held out his hand in friendship.

"Aye, but you stay here with me!" exclaimed Kamakau. "You can't leave and go sliding back through the black of this weather! Look, we bear straight on for the channel; we soon will be in the shelter of Tupia Bay."

"Not if you tack again," said Perique. "If you tack and run up past the harbor mouth, then I will have a chance to slip back into the Bay, and no one in Lanua will know that I have been outside at sea, to find my old friend Kamakau and talk with him. Then if I should face him on shore, afterwards, he would not speak of how I had come to see him before he ran into Tupia Bay."

"Ah, is it so?" said Kamakau. "How far away you think, Perique! How you take all the turns of the path until you are through the jungle! There is no other man like Perique. My head, now, would ache terribly before I could begin to make such long, winding plans. It would be easier to count all the fibers in a coconut than to learn the thoughts that are in your mind. Do you go? Will you have one drink of brandy, first?"

"If I were alone, yes," said Perique. "But there is the girl. And a man full of brandy is only half a brain and one hand, you know. Kamakau, when I stand up on the deck of your ship, I am standing on the matting in the middle of my own house. Look, the storm is dying since it found out that it could not keep Kamakau and Perique apart! Farewell! I shall see you soon. And keep your men from going ashore, for my sake!"

He ran aft. The sea was much quieter, now, and the sweep of the waves had fallen to a considerable degree. Still it was a most seamanly task to regain the small boat and cast off the rope. The huge thamakau at once went rushing ahead.

But almost at once, obedient to the wish of Perique, the huge canoe tacked.

That is a ticklish operation in a thamakau, because of course when a South Seas boat is sailed the outrigger never can be brought to leeward. Otherwise, the pressure of the wind would sink it under the waves and the larger craft would capsize. There have been such disasters, but not many, for the South Seaman is a master of his craft.

To change the course of the thamakau without alteration of the relation of the outrigger to the wind, the crew of the big boat now were turning the stern of the canoe into the bow. The steersman kept away until the wind was abeam, and the sheet was slacked until it was loosely wavering in the wind.

A number of strong men then ran into the bow, caught the yards, and carried them amidships. As they passed the mast the lower yard was let go, the sheet was passed around them, and the sail then turned inside out. They went on forward.

The mast began to incline after them. What was now the backstay was payed out carefully as the burden bearers went staggering forward.

In the meantime the weighty steering oar, a burden for three able men, had been shifted inboard and dragged aft. And in a little more than half a minute the big thamakau had hung fluttering its wings in the wind, and then started away with a rush on its new course.

The sharp commands from the chief blew down the wind to Perique through the midst of this delicate, swift maneuver. Now, as the big boat swept away, Perique could not help waving his hand, all had been done with such perfect and drilled precision.

His own small outrigger in the meantime was leaping for the mouth of the channel to Tupia Bay; and now it entered the dark mouth, and slipped rapidly between the headlands which lay on either side.

CHAPTER 25

Over the choppy waters of Tupia Bay the outrigger ran skipping and leaping and quenched its speed in the soft sand of the beach. As the girl and Perique sprang on shore, big Kohala loomed through the night, exclaiming: *"Hai . . . Konia!* Have you come back alive?"

"Perique keeps all the winds in his hands," said the girl. "He only lets them slip when he chooses."

Kohala helped carry the boat up the beach to its proper place. "Then," he was grunting, "he had better turn the wind about and let it blow him away from Tupia."

"How is that, Kohala?" asked Perique.

"They hunt for you through the town," said Kohala. "They have come to my house to look for you . . . but of course I had not seen you. You have been missed away from the Tavern, and fifty men are looking. Men with guns and without guns. Even the guards from the walls of the Tavern have joined in the hunt."

"When they find me, what will they do with me?" asked Perique.

"I cannot tell," said Kohala. "But they say that you walked through the wall of the Tavern and disappeared. I said nothing of the borrowed things you took from me."

"Konia," said Perique, "go back to your house. If I could have picked over all the men of Lanua, I could never have found a better eye or a quicker hand on the sheet of the sail. Except for you, the sharks would have had us both. Did you see the big black fins knifing through the water?"

"I had something better than sharks to think of," said the girl. "Besides, if they were there, it was because you called them, lord." She vanished at once into the night.

The dying wind still blew with force. A gust of rain beat against the face of Perique as he looked after the girl. The big drops, hard with speed, hurt his eyes.

"Take this skirt of yours, Kohala," he said, stripping it away. "And now help me to wring out my clothes that are tied around me. Take that end and twist . . ."

"*Ah hai!*" said Kohala, as the water gushed out. "You have been swimming!"

"That boat of yours is lucky. It will no more drown than a fish," said Perique.

"It is a good boat," said Kohala. "I used my adze to help in the hollowing of it. I chose the tree from which the log was cut. So the boat is like a child in my family."

"You have made it like Liho and Konia, straight and strong. Go back to your house now, Kohala. You have walked down on the beach to watch the waves jumping like black fish. But you did not see me here."

"I have not seen you at all, this night," said Kohala, laughing. "But where will you go?"

"Where my feet want to take me," answered Perique.

And since the wind was blowing him cold, he started off with a long, springing, tireless stride that carried him rapidly up the slope of Tupia hill.

When he came to the tavern of Bill Smith at the top of the hill, he took note of the high palisade. It was not true that all the guards had been called away to join the manhunt. Two of them were still parading up and down the wall against the moon and the storm in the sky.

Perique looked longingly at the little postern door which was let into the wall. The big gate was closed and locked at this hour, in this weather. And no one had the key to the little postern except Bill Smith himself and his old friend, Matthew Coffee.

Under the wall Perique waited patiently, sitting on his heels, staring upward as the guards passed at long intervals. He counted the seconds of those intervals. And in the middle of one of the pauses, the moon went dark with the rush of the last of the storm. Then, like a big cat, Perique went up the face of the palisade, finding fingerholds and toeholds here and there.

At the top he paused for an instant, saw the bowed heads of the guards pointed toward the wind, and let himself slide down the inner side of the wall, an elongating shadow which bunched up small at the bottom again.

He worked his way gradually, from the wall to a patch of brush, to a palm tree's trunk, and so to his own small terrace that offered shelter in front of his room.

He opened the door of his room and listened. He tasted the air with long breathing. He crossed the floor and slipped his hand over the bed. No one was there.

Without lighting a lamp, he found fresh water, washed the salt sea from his clothes, scrubbed the brown stain from face and body where the ocean might not have cleansed him, and then hung up his clothes with weights tied to stretch them so that they would dry without wrinkles, without shrinking.

After that, he went to bed, turned on his face, stretched out his tired arms crosswise, and fell sound asleep.

A squeak like that of a rat wakened Perique. He turned and found the full daylight; footfalls were racing away from his door.

He turned on his back, yawned, stretched, and picked up a package of cigarettes. He was lighting one of these when he heard a confused tumult pouring toward him. So he pulled a pillow under his shoulders and propped himself up in the bed.

The door, which had been pulled open a crack, was now thrust wide and the vast barrel of Bill Smith appeared at the entrance with a sawed-off shotgun in his hands.

"By golly, it's true!" said Bill Smith. "And here you are—! Here, boy, fetch me some gin and lemons—"

"I'll have rum," said Perique.

"And rum," called Bill Smith. "The rest of you, get out of here!"

The servants scattered. Their musical, excited chattering spread away across the terraces, wandered off dimly through the other rooms of the rambling tavern.

Bill Smith sat down, took off his hat, dropped it on the floor, and cut the sweat from his face with three strokes of a fat forefinger.

"Pretty near the death of me," said Bill Smith. "How did you do it? Was it the postern, Mr. Parry? Was it the postern that you managed to unlock and get out through?"

"I thought you said that you and the great man, Matthew Coffee, have the only keys to the postern?"

"A key could be stole," said Bill Smith. "Or it could be waxed and copied."

"Yes. A crook could do that," nodded Perique. He smiled straight into the eyes of Bill Smith. And Bill sighed and shook his head.

"How you managed to get out of the tavern last night is your own secret," admitted Bill.

"Did I go out from the tavern?"

"Did you which? Sure you did walk out. Or jump out, or burrow out. I don't know which, and you're not telling."

"I had a good deal to drink yesterday," said Perique.

"You have a lot every day," said Bill.

"I may have walked in my sleep," said Perique. "I don't know what else. But what's the matter, Bill? Did you miss me out of my room?"

"Did I miss you? Did Captain Wilshire miss you, too? I been half crazy trying to work it out, and I can't find a way. I've walked all around the palisade. There's not a place where the earth's been moved at the root of the poles. There's not a place where a rope could have been used for you to get over without being seen."

"I've always been a bit of a sleepwalker," said Perique. "I've got to change all that, Bill. I've got to see a doctor. One of these nights when I've fallen asleep, I'll be walking straight into trouble of some sort."

Bill Smith sighed very heavily. The boy with the drinks came in. Besides the rum and lemon and gin and siphon, he carried half of a big melon, the fruit deep and orange-red in color. This he offered as a breakfast to Perique who took it, spooned a bit from the center, and called to the boy to wait. Perique was mincing a bit of the melon between his teeth. He removed it from his lips and put the pulp back on the side of the dish.

"What's the matter?" asked Bill Smith.

"I'll eat later. Drink is what I need," said Perique. "Boy, bring in that caged parrot and put him on the chair by my bed. The eyes of a parrot are the brightest things in the world, Bill. They help to clear the sleep out of the head."

"That don't make much sense to me," said Bill. "But I've stopped trying to follow you, Mr. Parry."

The parrot having been brought in, Perique spooned a quantity of the melon from the rind and tossed it through the bars of the cage. The parrot twisted his head halfway

139

round and gave that red-fruited melon the unstinted consideration of one eye. Then he reversed the process. Afterward, he gobbled the melon and then hung himself by the claws and beak from the top wires of the cage.

Perique sipped lemon juice and rum.

And Bill Smith said: "They've gone to tell Captain Wilshire and the governor."

"The governor, too? I didn't know he was a friend of mine," said Perique.

Bill leaned far forward in his chair. "Don't be a damn fool, sir," he said. "They're gunna hang you or be damned, all of 'em."

"When I dance on the air, I hope I'll step high," said Perique.

"Why don't you clear out, sir?" said Bill Smith. "What is it that you're trying to do? What's there on Lanua for a man like you? I been saying that to myself all the while, that it ain't true, that you can't be here, that you wouldn't pick out a place so small as Lanua."

"There's a nice climate here, Bill," said Perique.

"Climate? Hell!" said Bill Smith.

Here the parrot swung down from the top wires of the cage and began to stretch its head through the bars toward the melon. Perique picked it up and began to eat with a fine appetite.

CHAPTER 26

Captain Wilshire would have taken his lieutenant with him, but Lieutenant Clifford had gone down to the beach where he had found certain deep footprints beside a fallen stone; he had called for help from a passing fisherman, and together, lifting the stone, they had discovered beneath it some fragments of newly burned iron.

140

That was why Lieutenant Clifford of the constabulary was not at hand to accompany his chief toward the tavern of Bill Smith. However, the squad of five men that followed the captain was enlarged by a curious crowd of whites and natives who strolled at a little distance to see the fun.

But there was no fun at all. Captain Wilshire, arriving at the tavern of Bill Smith, marched straight to the room of Perique and found him in calm conversation with the proprietor of the place.

"Mr. Parry," said the captain, "I have the honor to request you to appear with me before his excellency, the governor of Lanua. Kindly dress at once."

"I'm too tired to go," said Perique.

"I know you had a busy night," said the captain.

"Bill Smith has just been telling me that I must have gone walking in my sleep," said Perique. "He says that I was missed and away. Strange thing, captain, that I don't remember a thing about it."

Captain Wilshire had turned a bright red. He said: "One of these days we may be able to assist your memory of one of your nights, Mr. Parry."

"Matter of fact," said Perique, "I'm hardly ever bothered by sleepwalking. But I'm sorry that I wasn't here when you wanted me."

"I'm sure that you're sorry," said the captain. "The governor is sure, also. Will you rise and dress, Mr. Parry?"

"As soon as you've left the room and closed the door, captain," said Perique. "A man must have a decent privacy, you know."

"Decent privacy? Damn!" said the captain. "I'll not take my eyes from you, Mr. Parry, until you're in front of the governor himself."

"Very well," said Perique. "If there were an American consul on the island, I should appeal to him against this outrage. But if you want to watch me shave, that's your privilege."

He was standing presently in front of the square mirror stripped to the waist, and strapping his razor.

It was a big razor, with a deep blade, hollow-ground, the gray-blue of the steel glimmering.

Perique ran on: "Do you know about razors, captain?"

"I don't know. I'm not interested," said the captain.

"Ah, but you should be," said Perique. "Razors, captain, are like men. Some of them have the proper steel; some of them are poor soft stuff that wears away and won't hold an edge. But the true metal, in razors or in men, is what will take an edge and hold it, in spite of stiff beards, or Lanuan constabularies, or whatever."

"I have no interest in your remarks," said the captain.

"That's still a pity," said Perique. "I had a wise old uncle who told me, when I was a boy, to try to learn the best from everyone, no matter how strange."

"You seem to have hunted out the strange places for your studies, Mr. Parry. The governor is waiting all this time."

"Ah, but now the razor is sharp, and once the tool is ready, the work is done quickly. You see the beard is finished with a few gestures. Of course it might cut a little deeper."

"How much deeper?" asked the captain. "Has it ever cut as deep as a throat, Mr. Parry?"

"I'll ask it," said Parry, and flicked the edge of the razor with a forefinger. It gave out a light, sharp, high ringing note.

"What does it say?" asked the captain.

"You heard it with your own ears, captain," said Perique. "I wouldn't presume to know more than a captain of constabulary."

When they got out on the street, quite a crowd had gathered, and a deep-throated murmuring ran through the watchers as Perique stepped out smartly at the side of the captain, all agleam in well-pressed whites. He had a light bamboo walking stick in his hand and now and then he swung it with a flourish that made it flash out of sight for an

142

instant. It seemed plain that he was in high spirits.

At the brow of the hill, just outside the government building, Perique paused and screened his eyes with his hand so that he could look more easily through the bright steam of the morning mist. For the powerful sun was drawing up the rain of the night before to re-form in little clouds that blew rapidly across the sky. There in the bay lay the long length and the slanting mast and the loose, drying sail of the thamakau.

"A new boat in the harbor, isn't it?" asked Perique.

"Yes, a new boat," said the captain dryly.

"Ran in during the night, I suppose? Ran in to get out of the storm?"

"It had a purpose in coming to Tupia Bay," said the captain sternly, and led the way into the building. His armed men formed a close wall behind Perique as he mounted the stairs.

So they came into the room of the governor himself.

It ran right through the government building, with two large windows at each end, so that the sea breeze might have a full sweep when it chose to cool the fevered brain of the Honorable Irvine. The captain assigned a man to the guarding of each window.

Afterward he presented the prisoner to the governor.

The Honorable Irvine said: "Ah, Mr. Parry! Quite so . . . I remember your face . . . garden party . . . gin . . . I mean, I remember you—"

"Thanks," said Perique. "You remembered me well enough to want me this morning?"

"It's a hot day, isn't it?" said the Honorable Irvine. "If I had my way, we'd give up the foolish trousers and coats, starched and damned; we'd dress as God intended men to dress in the South Seas."

"In our skins," suggested Perique.

"Ha?" said the Honorable Irvine. "Skins? . . . Good . . . Yes . . . in our skins. Good idea, Wilshire, isn't it?"

"Yes, sir," said Wilshire coldly.

The governor was depressed by the gloom of his captain of constabulary.

"And so," said the governor, "we get on to . . . what do we get on to next, Wilshire?"

The captain of constabulary cleared his throat. "I believe, sir," he said, "that you wish to introduce Mr. Parry to an interview . . ."

"Interview with whom?" asked the governor. "Ah, yes. Now I remember. This is serious. A serious matter, Mr. Parry. . . . Wilshire, bring in our friend, will you? . . . But wait a moment. You have stated, Mr. Parry, that you were brought to Lanua in the boat of a native chief, a man named Kamakau. Is that correct?"

"I think I said that," said Perique.

"You only think?" demanded the captain savagely.

"What more can a poor man do?" answered Perique.

"Well, bring him in!" commanded the governor.

Here a side door was opened, and after a moment the huge bulk of Kamakau appeared. He had on, above bare legs, a beautiful stiffly starched white evening shirt with enormous pearl studs down the front of it and a faultlessly arranged white tie knotted in place. The huge neck of Kamakau somewhat overflowed this neckgear and kept him breathing hard. His old head seemed more cut off from the rest of his powerful body than ever. It was like a withered flower on a young stalk. He was so proud of his costume that as he walked he could not help looking down to the flaps of the shirt, which wavered just above his knees. His rod of authority was an ancient spear with a head shaped like a palm leaf and a heavy, short staff, engrossed with carvings so ancient that half the symbols no longer were understood. There was more divinity hedging that spear around than in the living person of the king.

"Now, Kamakau," said the captain loudly, "I am showing

144

you a person who claims that he was brought from Kandava here to Lanua by you, in person, on your own boat. Is there a scrap of truth in that?"

Kamakau looked slowly around the room, saw Perique, and extended his hand.

"Ah, my friend!" said he.

Captain Wilshire almost staggered. He got hold on the back of a chair and cried: "Kamakau, is it true? Did you bring him?"

"Certainly," said the chief.

"Why, look here, Wilshire," said the governor, "I thought that this was going to be a show? I thought it was going to be something worthwhile, and you've sold me. They're friends, the pair of them!"

"Conspiracy—infernal conspiracy to defeat the ends of proper law and order," panted the captain.

Kamakau, gripping Perique by both shoulders, was thundering out a great laughter that flooded the room and half maddened poor Captain Wilshire.

Somewhere on the stairs sharp voices of dispute were rising, cutting even into the august chamber of the governor.

"It's Clifford," muttered the captain. "He's the one who worked out the theory that—but Clifford *has* to be right."

"Captain Wilshire, Captain Wilshire!" said the Honorable Irvine, "I hope you haven't formed the habit of depending too much upon men who are too young. Lieutenant Clifford is a very young man, indeed. Someone do something about that racket out in the hall, please! It's bad enough to have to live in the heat of hell, without having the noise also."

At this moment there was a loud uproar breaking forth in the hallway; one of the guards at a window went to the hall door and opened it. At once there appeared in the doorway a man dressed in frightful rags, his body emaciated, his eyes glaring insanity. A pair of constabulary police were hanging onto him while he staggered and strained and argued, but as the door opened, he yelled in a frantic voice: "There! Get him! Nail him! It's Perique! It's that damned murdering, kidnaping Perique—"

Captain Wilshire uttered a faint moaning sound, which translated into the extreme of joy, and whirled with a good long .45 caliber revolver weighting down his hand. But the bulky form of Kamakau, that important native chief, obscured the vision of the captain. Perique was somewhere behind the chief and speeding for a window.

"Stop him! Shoot him down!" roared Wilshire, dodging to the side to get a fair shot at the fugitive.

When he had the window in clear line for his shooting, he saw his constabulary officer at that window in the act of shooting just as his gun was knocked upward.

The hand of Perique at the same moment clicked against the jaw of the man, then caught the falling bulk of the body and drew it into the window sill. Over that window sill Perique slipped and dropped from sight.

The loosely spilling body of the constabulary officer that had made a shield between Perique and the guns of the law, now slumped to the side and was about to dive headlong from the window when the running captain caught him by the legs and dragged him back to fall safely to the floor.

"It's all right," said the Honorable Irvine. "Perique's down there with a broken neck or smashed legs. It's twenty-five feet from that window to the ground, captain, and—"

Captain Wilshire whirled from the window and began to scream out orders.

"Get down to the street! He's gone! The whole lot of you on the run. Tomason, get to the beach and turn out the guard there. Willett, start the forest patrol around the edge of the forest and keep the men riding. There's a thousand honest pounds on his head. . . ."

These wild commands started a stampede among the men in the governor's office, and as the rest swept out through the door and went crashing down the stairs, like so many bounding stones, the Honorable Irvine rose from his chair at last and walked in a leisurely manner to the window through which Perique had disappeared.

The stunned constabulary officer, in the meantime, was sitting up, groaning with every breath he drew.

"Come, come, my friend," said the governor. "A little clip on the chin like that hasn't done you any real harm. . . ."

And he stepped past the fellow to look down from the open window.

In fact, it was two stories from the ground, and that ground was hard-beaten. As well, almost, to drop on a flat rock. It made the feet of the Honorable Irvine tingle to contemplate that distance, merely. He saw the constabulary men issue into the street from the government building. He heard the shouting of that deadly formula: "A thousand pounds' reward . . ." He saw men mounting on mules and horses and rattling off at full gallop.

"Ha!" said the Honorable Irvine. "This is as good as a long drink . . . poor Wilshire!"

And he stepped back from the window, laughing. His laughter stopped as he stared into the pale agonized face of the constabulary officer. The man was supporting his jaw with a tender hand, and very distinctly the governor heard the grating noise of the two edges of a broken bone.

The Honorable Irvine remembered the blow. He had seen it struck while he was in a ringside seat, so to speak, and it had been a little, short flick of arm and shoulder, with the hand moving not a foot in distance.

A very neat little left hook such as might make a boxer blink a bit if he were on the receiving end. But in this case —it was very odd—for the constabulary officer was a big fellow, thick-necked, with a gorilla-like ridge of bone above the eyes, and one of those short, wide, heavily made jaws which are ideally constructed to receive and withstand

147

shocks.

The Honorable Irvine made a soft, rapid clucking sound of the tongue against the palate of his mouth. He shook his head a little and lightly dusted his two hands together.

CHAPTER 27

Perique, dropping from the window of the government house, slid to the earth past the nose of an islander who pulled a knife and made a half-stab into the air with it as instinctively as a cat makes a tentative stroke with its paw.

Perique, slumping loosely to the ground to break the force of the long fall, rolled away from the flash of that knife and came to his feet covered with dust. Something in the look of him as he rose made the native turn and flee. But he need not have feared, for the head of Perique had struck the ground hard enough to daze him. He staggered toward a haze in which one mule looked like two. Behind and above him, voices were yelling; a thunder of footfalls had started descending the stairs inside the government building.

Perique reached for the halter of the mule. When his fingers grasped the rope, his wits cleared a little. He saw that the beast was a scrawny, poor creature but there was no time to select a more promising mount. He jumped onto the back of the gray-haired old veteran and drove his heels against the bony flanks.

For answer, he got a racking, shortened, hobbling excuse for a gallop that took him around the next corner out of sight of all except the upper forehead of the government house. The moment he was off the single street of Tupia's civilization, a jumble of native huts, big and small, surrounded him. And from behind, he heard the sound of the pursuit begin and explode outward. They had horses under them, those fellows of the constabulary, and they were traveling three feet to his one.

He knew, instantly, that he never would reach the edge of the town, to hide himself in the cultivated fields or to get farther on into the comparative safety of the great jungle. Or would even the jungle be safe when the Lanuans were sure to go searching everywhere, for the sake of the big price on his head, like so many secret brown snakes?

He pulled the mule to the side. It stumbled on both knees so that he almost fell off over its head.

He stepped off the back of that poor wooden thing and watched it go rocking away at its pitiful canter. Hoof-beats were rushing toward him. He leaped back under the shadow of widely projecting thatch and saw a half-breed member of the constabulary spurring furiously by with a light rifle gripped in his right hand. The fellow was shouting in the native tongue: "Perique! Perique! The price of a thousand pigs for him. Who's seen him go? The big man of the tavern . . ."

The door of the native house against which he had shrunk stood open, dark as the mouth of a cave, and glancing inside it he could see no one. He leaped over the threshold, scanned the place with a hasty glance, and then went up the center post of the building like a cat.

It was a house of the bigger and better sort. The center post itself was half the trunk of a heavy tree and on it rested the ends of four huge beams which had been roughly squared with the adze. These beams, extending to the four parts of the circular house, gave firm strength to its wall. A secondary post rose, continuing the first one but much lighter, and this was the support for the dome of high thatch that descended on all sides over a framework of interwoven branches. This made a house secure against anything except the most violent hurricane.

And as Perique stretched himself out on one of the cross-beams that reached out toward the door of the hut, he blessed the ambition of the builder who had given the house such a massive skeleton. The beam was so wide that, if Perique put his arms out above his head, he could hardly be seen by people on the ground beneath.

Here he heard a scratching noise, and saw the spurt of the flame of a match in a corner of the room. It was an old man who had been sitting there all the while and who had seen, of course, the entrance of the stranger. Now the flame of the match, as he lighted a pipe, showed to Perique the flat, battered face and the gray head of old Maku, who had recognized him on that first night at the house of Kohala. Maku who had traveled so far and so wisely!

Perique sat up on his rafter, but here several people came sweeping through the door of the hut, a woman, a boy of a dozen years, and an athletic man of middle age with a shotgun in his hands.

Thunder, like a well-timed stage effect, boomed suddenly and close overhead.

"I want the extra cartridges, father," said the big man. "Where are they?"

"It is going to rain," said Maku calmly. "Why should you go hunting birds or pigs when it is going to rain?"

"Perique is in Tupia! Perique has been found, and has run away. The big man of the tavern. That is Perique, with a thousand pounds' reward on his head. *Ah hai!* I shall use the money to buy a great thamakau and afterwards we shall live like kings of the island. He is here in Tupia; he cannot escape; the horsemen are guarding the edges of the town! Where are the cartridges, father? *Hai!* Quick! By hundreds they are searching; even the boys have taken guns to go hunting!"

"Listen!" said the old man, lifting his withered hand.

And at that moment the first of the rain struck Tupia. It struck like the flat of a vast hand. A creaking went through the domed thatch of the house. Dark of twilight filled the doorway, but beyond it, Perique could see the bright rain-dust flying in the street.

The peal of the thunder split open the brain. A new torrent rushed down with the first, striking the top of the house a second blow.

"You see, Palakee," said Maku, "that this is no weather for hunting."

Big Palakee went to the door of the house and glowered at the downpour.

"Perique is taboo," he said. "Also, he is a great wizard, and he has made this rain. But this is no weather for hunting."

"Except inside the house," said Maku, lifting his head and gazing at the place where Perique lay stretched out on the beam of wood.

Perhaps he saw the gleam of the revolver in the hand of Perique. At any rate, he looked down quickly again.

Palakee said: "I *would* search the house except that you've been here all the time."

"Old men have sleepy eyes," said Maku.

"Not you," answered Palakee. "No cat ever slept so lightly . . . *Ai! Ai!* What a rain!"

He turned back into the house and began to stride gloomily up and down the strips of matting that covered the floor. The boy sat on his heels and watched the rain sluicing down the street. A woman came running in with a cloth folded over her head. She threw it off. It struck the center post with a splash. She began to pant and laugh at once. Time had done its usual work on her, turning her face flabby, stretching out her mouth, narrowing her eyes under the fleshy weight of the lids.

"They are galloping everywhere, the men with the guns," she said. "But now they will only get wet. They will find nothing. If only the guards can keep him from getting down to the sea or away to the forest."

"Even if he were a fish, the Lanuans would catch him; even if he had the wings of a parrot, we would find a way of putting him in a cage," said Palakee. "A thousand pounds! Do you know what that much money means? Five hundred guns like this; or a thousand pigs. Enough pigs to feed a big army of hungry men for a week! A thousand pounds! What a disgrace if the men of Lanua let him get away! But we shall have him!"

He turned to the woman and asked for food. She picked up firewood and began to arrange it for cookery. Four small iron pots hanging from a single frame she pushed over above the wood.

The boy said, from the doorway: "If he is a wizard and can make the rain come down, can't he make himself invisible and walk away?"

"If he could walk invisible, why does he need the rain?" asked Palakee.

Something splashed up to the entrance as the woman lighted her fire; she commenced to cut up vegetables to put into the pots. And now a dripping man pushed across the threshold. He was in the uniform of the constabulary. This was one of the pure-blood natives who had been admitted to the picked force.

"Are you here, Maku?" he asked. "Let me come in and dry myself for a little while, will you?"

The head of a horse poked through the entrance, with pricking ears.

"Come in," said Maku. "Come in and welcome. But I should think that all of you riders would be out guarding the edge of the town to see that he doesn't escape."

There was a wooden tub for waste and scraps, in a corner of the room. A chicken sat on the rim of it, picking at bits of food. It only moved over a little when the constabulary man pulled off his shirt and wrung it, letting a gush of water pour into the tub.

He was explaining: "You see how the thing is? They keep a few of us inside Tupia. Suppose that he's in the town and found, then we can run quickly with our horses to the place and put an end to him. The rest of the riders make a patrol and go around and around Tupia."

The boy said: "What a great man he must be to be worth

so much money! What has he done besides witchcraft?"

"Isn't that enough?" demanded Palakee. "Think of a man who can make the rain fall like this so that he may get away! Besides, he is a great killer of men. When he sails the sea, he calls for the wind he wants, and immediately it blows for him. He whistles, and the fish come to his hook."

The woman said: "He has been seen riding on the back of a shark, leaning against the curve of the big fin. Whales have thrown up ambergris so that it would wash ashore at his feet."

Here the horse of the constabulary officer, compelled by the whipping of the rain, edged his way into the house of Maku and stood turning his head in fear of the humans and the strangeness of this shelter. No one paid any attention to the horse, because of the intense interest in the topic of Perique.

In the meantime, his place on the beam was no longer tenable. The fire had been burning during the interval and the smoke which should have been drawn up through the ventilation hole at the top of the roof was, instead, beaten back again by the intense weight of the rain. So that a white cloud began to form at the top of the thatch, gradually building, swelling lower and lower until its billows reached the place where Perique was lying.

He put a handkerchief over his mouth and nose, closed his eyes, and turning on his breast he began to inch forward along the beam.

The smoke which was choking him was also enough to make him invisible. It was, in addition, a shield to old Maku, who now yelled out: "There—up there in the smoke—*there* is the thousand pounds we want! There is Perique! Watch, and you'll see him climb down the center post. Have your gun ready. Don't try to capture him. But shoot! shoot!"

The woman, the moment she heard this, began to scream, an endless sound as though she were able to live and give tongue without breathing. Her husband started shouting—

orders to the constabulary to stand by him, orders to the boy to get the horse out of the house.

Then Perique, leaning down from the billows of the smoke, saw the horse at the door as the lad caught the bridle reins and turned the animal toward the street.

He loosed his hold on the beam and dropped to the floor.

The men in the house had their attention so firmly fixed on the center post that Perique actually reached the ground behind the back of the constabulary officer. It was the boy who saw the long body drop out of the smoke. He screamed, leaping back from the head of the horse; and Perique was instantly in the saddle, flattening his body along the neck of the bay as it leaped for the street, wild with alarm.

One gun exploded with a roar. The two barrels of the shotgun had been fired, and the load went crash into the thatch; the buckshot hissed over the head of Perique as the horse struck the flowing mud of the street.

CHAPTER 28

Report of Officer Tomi Kalino, of the Lanua Constabulary, Tupia Station:

I, the undersigned, Tomi Kalino, sergeant of the Lanua Constabulary, declare that on Tuesday, the twenty-second day of the month, the following events came under my observation:

You see, when the alarm came about Perique I was on duty at Government House and my horse was at the hitching rack in front of the building. I got to the horse on the run and cut the halter rope and jumped into the saddle.

Everybody was shouting: "Perique!" and I shouted it, too. The order was to get to the outside of Tupia and watch the edge of the city so that Perique could not get away into the forest. After I got past the edge of the city, the rain came down, smash. I mean, the rain began to fall heavily. It got so heavy that you couldn't see ten steps away, hardly; and I had to keep watching to make sure that as I rode up and down I always could see the next men on post there. It was as dark as just after sundown before you can see stars. I got wet like I had dived into water. I kept the lock of my rifle covered all the time, though.

After a long time, I thought that the rain got less hard. Then I could hear a gunshot in Tupia. Afterwards, there was yelling. Everybody in Tupia seemed to be yelling all at once. The sound came rushing out. It seemed to be running straight at me. I could hear people yelling: "Perique! Perique!" And I got my rifle at the ready and waited. I faced right in toward Tupia and sat there in the saddle. I watched the long grass and every bush in front of me so that nobody could slip past.

Then all at once something dark jumped up in front of me, out of the grass, or from behind a bush. It must have been magic. Nothing was there. And then a man was jumping at me. He came in from the left and I swung my rifle across the pommel of the saddle and fired. But as he jumped at me, he waved his hands, and the horse swerved, so that I missed. That was more magic. Because my horse is very gun-wise and never is afraid.

I knew that my first bullet had missed and I tried to shoot again, but there wasn't time. The man jumped up onto the horse and caught hold of me.

Now I can prove by what happened that Perique is a magician. I have a black-and-blue bruise on both wrists and another above my right knee and another at the back of my neck. Those are the places where he caught hold of me.

I am a big man. Everybody knows that I am the best wrestler on Tupia Beach. But when he caught hold of me, one hand went numb and then the other. He took the gun away from me and I was like a woman. I could not keep a grip on it. He dragged me off the horse. I tried to fight. I tried to pull out my knife but he caught my right wrist and my fingers opened of their own accord and the gun dropped. I had to stand there and look at him.

I had seen him in Tupia, walking up the street. But when I saw Perique there in the rain he was much bigger. He was so big I felt like a child.

He spoke to me in good Lanuan. No white man could speak such good Lanuan except he was a wizard.

He said: "Now what am I to do with you? Slide a knife between your ribs—or will you give me your promise not to make a sound for one minute after I ride on?"

I said that Tomi Kalino would be no good for anything if he were dead, and that is true. I promised that I would count to one hundred if he didn't kill me, before I gave the alarm.

He looked at me for a minute. I saw that he was ready to kill me and I closed my eyes. When I opened them again, he was gone, my horse was gone. They had vanished. A wizard can make himself vanish, but I never heard of a horse vanishing before. That shows what a strong wizard Perique is.

I started to count, the way I had promised. He had left a spell on me that made me very sick at the stomach, but I kept on counting as far as I could, that was up to nineteen. I counted that far twice. Then I yelled as hard as I could. After a while, people came and I told them what had happened. They rode on past me. Captain Wilshire was very angry.

156

I say that Perique is a terrible wizard and that I am not afraid of anybody who is just a man.

All that I say is the truth.

(signed)

Tomi Kalino.

Report of Benedict Lawson, in brief:

When I heard in Kandava about the man who had appeared in Lanua, I just had an idea that it might be Perique. Because I knew that he was the sort that showed up when you never expected him.

I always hated Perique since the day that he robbed me. The way was this. It was down near Apia. There had been a ship went down the day before in a hurricane. It was the *Silvester B. Jones,* of the Jones and Jones trading company. It hit the reef and went down and me and two friends were the first there. We kept diving for an hour before the natives began to come out and dive, too.

We got hold of a lot of good stuff before the natives showed up and we took the boat back to the beach and put our loot out on the sand. There were clothes and some good guns and a lot of tackle of one sort or another, and I got into the captain's cabin myself and almost drowned before I found his money and got back to the surface nearly dead.

We sat around the beach and argued till dark about the way we would divide things. And while we were still arguing, a big man walked in out of the darkness and took the money off the rock where it was lying. He said: "If I don't take this, you boys will be cutting throats because of it, before long."

That was Perique. We all jumped for him, but everything went wrong and he got away. I mean, he was so

157

lucky that we had to run for our lives, all except Stephen Rafferty, who wasn't able to run, and who came after us, crawling, and yelling for help.

So I hated Perique from that day on because he's a dirty thief. When I heard about the big man that had come to Tupia and some of the things he had done, I said to myself that it might be Perique, and I arranged so I could go to Tupia, not saying anything to anybody except that I had a big suspicion. I landed from the *Flying Spray* and that boy called Liho, that you caught, met me and told me he would show me a short-cut to Government House, but going up the hill a man jumped me from behind. I mean, I just had time to turn around and then I caught it on the chin.

It was Perique that smacked me down. I know because of the size of him. And I know by the way his knuckles fitted onto my chin. It was like being dicked by a walking-beam. I went out like a light and when I came to, sort of flickering, that Liho was there, and my arms were tied, and he led me along by a string into the jungle and up through the woods. I go so tired I almost died and then he got behind me and drove me ahead of him and whanged me with a stick all the way to the house of a Lanuan called Marika who is Liho's uncle.

Marika and his wife and his two daughters and his son all came out of their house and laughed at me. I heard Liho talk to them and speaking about Perique and they all were scared, because Perique is taboo.

They took and kept me, and Liho went away. Marika and his people were cruel to me. You wouldn't believe that dirty islanders could treat a white man like they did. I mean, what are white men going to amount to in the South Seas when cheap, common Lanuans can take and make a man climb the trees to get the coconuts, and work like a slave shredding the meat fine, and beat the tappa for cloth, and rub the cooking pots clean with sand? If you took and hanged Marika and his whole family, it would be a good example, I humbly submit. The worst was that they kept laughing at me all the time.

Twice I tried to run away. Once Marika and his son came after me and caught me, because no white man can run like an islander. They beat me and brought me back. The next time I tried to run away, the men didn't bother. Marika just called out and his two big girls, fast as greyhounds, lighted out after me and caught up with me. I tried to beat them off, but one of them got behind me with a stick and hit me till I gave up.

But finally I got a chance one day to slip a couple of coals out of the fire into the thatch of the house and the wind blew it into a fire. While Marika and his family were busy saving things out of the house, I got away and came as fast as I could to Tupia. You know that I almost came in time to catch Perique.

All I claim is half the reward when Perique is caught, because I guess nobody has tried as hard as me to catch him and nobody has suffered so much. Besides, you never would have known he was on the island if I had not come all the way over from Kandava.

(signed)

Benedict Lawson.

Report of Lieutenant Lawrence Clifford of the Lanuan Constabulary:

I, the undersigned, on the twenty-second instant, pursuing investigations of the sinking of the *Nancy Lee* and the brutal murder of the lighthouse keeper, was attracted by certain signs on the Tupia Beach and discovered under a stone fragments of small iron, obviously the binding of such a box as a sea-chest. One of those fragments had upon it the initials "H. L." and I presumed at once that I had come upon relics of the dead man, Harrison Lee.

The secreting of these bits of iron led me to believe that the sea-chest, perhaps, had been burned somewhere in the vicinity, and pursuing my search into the forest I finally discovered small, well-covered traces of fire. In an adjoining clearing a wink of light drew my eye upwards and I saw a knife sticking at a great height into the trunk of a tree. I was able to climb to the place and withdraw a knife only slightly rusted from the tree. The knife had upon it, also, the initials "H. L." and has since been identified, positively, by the daughter of Harrison Lee as having been his property.

The conclusions I draw are that Harrison Lee was not, as has been suspected, drowned in the sinking of the *Nancy Lee,* but that he was murdered after his arrival on shore with his sea-chest. He was perhaps the solitary survivor of the ship.

His murderer, perhaps maddened with pleasure by the killing and by the possession of the plunder of the sea-chest, hurled away the knife in an excess of delirious celebration. This act having restored him partially to his senses, he then set about covering up the traces of the crime with a good deal of cunning.

The body of Harrison Lee may be discovered at almost any moment. The search for him continues busily.

It is unnecessary to point out that the hunted criminal, James Parry, otherwise known as Perique, had in his possession the coat of Harrison Lee when he first appeared in Tupia. At that time I favored his arrest, but the letter of the law would not allow that procedure.

(signed)

Lawrence Clifford,
Lieutenant of Constabulary, Lanua.

Proclamation by the Governor, the Honorable Irvine Glastonbury:

Be it known to all by these presents that I, Irvine Glastonbury, Governor of His Majesty's Island of Lanua, do proclaim and offer a reward of one thousand pounds in addition to the thousand pounds already standing for the capture, alive or dead, or information leading to the capture of, James Parry, alias Perique.

Irvine Glastonbury,
Governor of Lanua.

CHAPTER 29

Perique paused to rest, when he was halfway up the side of the mountain. Climbing under that broiling sun was hard work, even for him. Now he sat down and watched the blue of the ocean through the trunks of the great palms. The edge of the forest, through which he had just come, was a steaming wall of green in the lower ground.

Perique, stretching himself on his back, closed his eyes and drew one of those great breaths which take the place of a yawn and stretch and give a comfortable tug to the spine.

But he had hardly shut his eyes when some incredibly small sound disturbed him, and instantly he was sitting up.

A coconut whanged on the ground close beside him, and a moment later he heard the scuttering claws of a great land-crab coming down the trunk of the palm.

When it reached the bottom of the trunk, it stood for only a moment to consider the man. Then it advanced with mighty claws poised, open and ready for attack. It was a two-foot giant, one of those insatiable eaters that will consume three good coconuts in a single day, and remain equally ravenous for the morrow!

"Brother," said Perique, laughing, "if I knew your drilling system, I'd borrow it and take it home with me."

But instead of starting to work on his prize, the crab lifted

161

the ponderous weight of the coconut and carried it off on his queer, bending, staggering legs. Somewhere in the distance he would strip its fibers away and commence his precise task of boring through the hard wall of the fruit at that point where the stem attachment had left it a little less tough. Perique, watching it out of sight, was about to lie down again when he saw the danger coming.

It was not from one side only. But, untouched by any wind, the tall grass on his left began to wave, and at the same time a dozen men broke out of the jungle at the bottom of the slope and began to run toward him, swerving to left and then to right partly to disturb his aim if he fired, and partly to take some of the angle out of the climb.

Perique, rising to one knee, glanced rapidly about him. But there was no time to consider ways and means. Out of the tall grass on his left a score of armed Lanuans rushed toward him. Some of them were firing as they ran. They were not a hundred yards off.

Perique fled up the slope. There was no other course. Rising toward the crest of the peak, of course he narrowed the ground over which the pursuit would have to search, but he was too closely driven to throw them off the trail by trickery.

A screen of huge rocks helped him for a moment, but when he had clambered through them, he saw only a great forest of canes twenty and thirty feet high, crackling and groaning softly together as the wind swayed them.

Perique made one pause, looked desperately upward, and then plunged into the brake.

At the margin it was fairly open and he could race on, dodging like a football runner, but presently he came to a portion where he had to lunge with his full weight, sidewise. And still the canes thickened until he was able to work on only by slow inches.

Behind him, he heard the voices of the hunters; he heard the crash of them striking the outer edge of the brake.

So he paused for a moment to listen and to consider. Then

he heard the crashing of the canes as strong knives began to cleave through them, clearing at least one path.

They might take a simpler way and set fire to the brake—but perhaps the canes were too green to burn. In any case, if they could surround the brake, they had him neatly trapped. And in the meantime they could cleave a path here and there, searching for him.

He could be glad of only one thing, that the noise they made would cover the sounds of his own efforts. So he pressed forward again.

It was hot beyond endurance, a thick, close, humid heat, as though a great animal were breathing in his face. His lungs began to burn to the bottom. The first sickness of exhaustion entered at his knees.

He went on with a steady, patient effort, not with hope, but with despair steadily locked back behind his teeth. Thirst began to dry up his throat, but thirst was an old familiar, almost a chosen companion on many a desperate voyage.

He noticed, presently, that he had reached a place where only his upper body encountered heavy resistance. Below the knees or from about that point he could feel nothing and therefore he shrank down until he found himself in an irregular sort of tunnel which worked back and forth through the lower canes. It was rank with the smell of pigs and apparently the wild swine which ran through the interior of Lanua had kept open this difficult passage through the brake as it grew tall and strong.

The heat was less. The light was a strange green dusk. And he found that with only an occasional halt to wriggle past a protruding root he was able to get forward on hands and knees quite smoothly.

There was one danger. The canes had been forced aside at the bottom, but the result was that they wove together above his head, at the top of the tunnel, in an impenetrable roof. He could not turn back. He could not rise and stand. There was no exit except straight on through this strange little tunnel.

Something grunted softly, ahead of him. He had a glimpse through the green twilight of flashing eyes and heard the turning and the flight of a pig. He could make out the quick patter of those small hoofs very dimly through the noise of the cane-cutting in the distance; but it was very easy to hear the whining, continual grunt that now came toward him.

Bigger feet made heavier impacts on the ground, and right on Perique came a full-grown wild boar with a great mane rising over the hump of its shoulders, and its immense, low-swung head garnished with a crooked pair of tusks.

Perique knew what this meant. You may frighten a lion or a tiger even out of its lair, but when a wild boar feels that his privacy has been infringed upon, he will charge the throned lightnings themselves.

Perique, lunging forward, twisted onto his back and one elbow, and stabbed upward with the knife he had drawn. The knife edge slashed right across the jowl of the boar.

He drew back. His grunting ceased. He commenced to champ his jaws together and a stream of bloody froth poured from his mouth. Right and left he tried his tusks. They split the heavy canes like paper. Then he rushed Perique.

No stabbing from beneath was possible, now. In that first stroke, Perique had hoped to drive upward until the blade touched a vital spot or severed the windpipe; but the boar charged now with his formidable head almost touching the ground.

Up rose Perique until his back crushed against the roof of the tunnel. In so doing, he was exposing all the soft of his belly to those rending tusks, but he had seen where his only chance might lie. The picture of the stroke burned brilliantly before his mind—then he stabbed far out and down, driving the needle-sharp point into the hide just in front of the shoulder. Through that tough skin, through masses of muscle tough as gristle, the blade drove, grated heavily against bone, and plunged on into the vitals.

The swinging tusk of the boar slashed Perique's arm open to the bone. One stroke, and then the beast fell on its knees. Perique drew back, tugged the knife out of the wound, and blessed with all his soul that matador who far off in Madrid had inspired him by the delicate, swerving grace of his art in giving death to the bulls.

The boar, silently, as he had fought, was dying. And as he died, he still strove to battle. The last convulsion stiffened his knees. He heaved himself from the bloody ground and lurched a step before the life went out of him. And so, slumped limp at the feet of Perique, the boar died. His fall drove a last grunt from his nostrils. One rear hoof kicked out feebly, twice.

On the haunch of the brute Perique sat down, ripped his shirt into strips, and bound the wound.

If he did not bleed to death, he would have to draw the bandage tight. If he drew it tight, he would lose the use of his right arm until the cut could be properly dressed. And to be left-handed on such a day as this!

He drew the bandage tight. It seemed to him that he was driving the tusk of the boar home against the bone anew, the pain was so great. But the bleeding stopped. He crawled on again, wriggling slowly, for he had only the force of his left arm to lift him, now, and even those long snakes of muscle which robed his shoulder began to ache as though they were seized with a cramp. He had a rest every minute for a few seconds. Darkness came over his eyes with the effort. At last, lifting himself after an instant of repose, a flare of brilliance struck into his eyes. He discovered that he had crawled whole yards out of the tunnel in the blindness of his exhaustion.

Sitting up, he looked eagerly about him. The blindness receded. His eyes cleared, but only after that did the roaring of the blood in his ears diminish so that he could hear the crackle of the falling cane under the knives of the natives; their voices, too, were drawing perilously near. But there seemed no possible escape for him except to turn back into the brake. For the canes grew to almost the edge of the mountain's brow.

Left and right they advanced to the very lip of a cliff; only in this spot they receded a little and left a small clearing which the wild swine had used as a perfectly safe retreat. It was heavily littered with their dung.

He crawled to the edge of the rock. A low, booming voice rose to him out of the depths where a waterfall, diminished to a meager flash by distance, dropped over the edge of a rock in the midst of a narrow gorge. That meager run of water had chiseled away at the rock for millions of years, hewing out its small channel, and the eye of Perique thickened with that hollow profundity of air. Somewhere in the depths a bird's whistle was sounding. It seemed to him an exquisite mockery of music.

He rose and turned. To go back into the cane was the only way left to him if he wished to keep his life. But that would not preserve him long. The knives of the hunters would reach him soon, and then they would shoot him like a poor cringing dog caught in a thicket.

He took up his life in the flat of his hand and looked at it, so to speak. Whatever that life had been, there had been no cringing.

He put away the knife, sticky with his own blood and that of the dead boar. There was the revolver, still, and six shots in its chambers. Those six shots he intended to use, and get a man for each of them. The day that they captured Perique and earned a fortune for the work would be a time for the Lanuans to remember; they might even say at the end of the hunt that the prize had hardly been worth the expense of the getting.

So he prepared himself, taking one long breath with relish to the bottom of his lungs and balancing the gun carefully. His right hand, that had the real brains in it, was lost to him. But his left-handed shooting might be more than the Lanuans would relish. There would even be a hope of driving them back except that the calm, nervy Englishmen, Clifford and Wilshire, were certain to be on hand to set the natives a stern example.

The bird-whistle out of the ravine sounded on a higher, a more thrilling note. He turned to look into the chasm again, handling the terrible depths calmly, as one may do when life is about to end. And so it was that he saw, halfway up the opposite slope of the gorge, the slender brown figure of a girl with the sun flashing on her. Even from that distance her beauty came to him like a song. It was Konia, still whistling, waving desperately to the left as though she wanted him to go in that direction.

CHAPTER 30

Perique waved. The sun flickered on the body of Konia as she leaped with happiness; and still she waved him to the left. To the very edge of the canebrake, where it joined the lip of the cliff, she urged him on and then struck both hands down as though encouraging him to descend.

Descend how? The brow of the cliff dropped with hardly a wrinkle, and almost sheer.

Behind him the voices of the Lanuans pressed closer. He could make out the commands of Captain Wilshire in incredibly bad Lanuan dialect. Still, down the gorge, the girl waved him to descend, down and farther to the left.

He dropped to his knees and thrust his head well out, clinging with his left hand to the canes. He could see, now, what she meant. The wild swine who used that high place for a shelter had not gone through the canebrake alone but some of them, at least, had found a zigzag way down the dizzy face of the rock. He could see the trail etched dimly, faintly worn in the solid stone by the feet of the pigs. Far, far down, he now saw one little black form running, leaping from side to side almost like a mountain goat. But a four-footed wild beast can go where hardly a bird would dare to follow.

If he had had two hands for the work, it might have been possible. He pushed the revolver suddenly into his clothes and crept around the edge of the canes. The footholds were on the slant and yet he kept a toehold. And his big left hand, finding crevices or small projections, was the thing that anchored him to some safety.

He looked up. Thirty feet of stone staggered above him toward the sky. Whatever he could do in the descent, he could not manage to make the ascent again; and already his left arm and shoulder ached with the labor.

The worst part was the necessary turn of the head to look down into the abyss and try to search out the proper trail that skimmed the verge of it. He went down steadily. The sun, focusing on him against the cliff, scalded his body, naked to the waist as it was, and put teeth into the pain of his wound.

He began to move automatically. A separate mind seemed to direct his feet. They were finding what his eyes had not seen; his left hand moved rhythmically, always from one handhold to another. He was having luck, he felt. There was no skill of mountaineering in this, but only blind luck.

Voices boomed above him through the empty gorge, struck the opposite side, echoed back in confusion. He paused and looked up. Small figures were up there, black against the sky, half a dozen of them, barely glimpsed.

He clung close to the rock, breathing hard. Would they use bullets, or would they merely stone him off the precipice?

The voices diminished. There was no whip sting of a bullet through his flesh, no cracking echo of a rifle shot. If they had not seen him, were they turning back into the canebrake again?

Here he heard a confusion of shouting, muffled, far overhead. That might mean the discovery of the dead body of the boar.

And now, to his right, the trail which the wild swine had

168

found broadened to a path of incredible ease and safety—a broad highway fully a foot in width! He merely needed to angle his body toward the cliff and then step out with a full stride.

Coolness washed like water over his body and burning head. The shadow from the opposite rock had risen and covered him. And the song of many deep voices that rose from the ravine was the shouting of the waterfall.

He looked up, but there was no sign of guns peering down after him. Instead, a cloud of smoke was crowning the cliff and blowing aslant down the wind.

They were trying fire, at last, on the brake; and the strength of the wind was making the flames consume even that green food. In the meantime, the anxious watchers waited for the quarry to come dashing out through the smoke in a last struggle for life. They were nursing their rifles, hungrily. They were counting the good, broad, bright pieces of gold.

He reached level ground so suddenly that his knees wavered under him. The air was cold and damp with the tossing spray of the waterfall; and through its calling a smaller voice came to him. It was from Konia. She was running, as fearless as though her extended, balancing arms were wings, across the very edge of the falls, springing from one slippery stone to another, and yet seeming to give no heed at all to her footing but laughing happily toward Perique.

Then she was before him, putting her hands against the blackened crusts of blood that covered his body.

"What have they done to you, lord?" cried Konia. "Is it a bullet? You have bound your arm too hard. It is black-purple. The arm is dying. It will have to be cut away. *Ai! Ai!* What is a man when his right hand is gone from him? Half his soul is in the right hand of a brave man!"

"It was a boar's tusk that ripped me up," said Perique. "Show me a path out of the valley. Get me to a place where you can sew up the wound."

"Lie down here and rest. Your legs are shaking."

"They will come around from the top of the rock and search for my body here," said Perique. "They are burning the canebrake and when my body is not found in the ashes, they will come down here to see where I threw myself over the rock. How can they tell that Konia and the wild pigs would show me the way down the rock?"

He laughed a little, and looked back up the cliff, half awash with shadow, half brilliant with the sun. Even from this point of view the trail was very dim, dropping in long strokes or short, faintly marked across the face of the rock.

"Come, then!" said Konia.

She pulled his left arm over her shoulder and gripped the hand hard. "Put a great deal of weight on me. I can carry it," she said. "Ah, lord, when they hunted you through the highlands like a pack of dogs, I followed. I saw them from the edge of the jungle charge on you and drive you into the canes. So I came around the shoulder of the mountain to this valley; and so I saw you standing on the edge of the rock; and I saw, also, the little dim mark of the trail which even a cat would be afraid to try, but my lord has no fear. There is still an ache in my throat from whistling so long and high. But at last my lord saw me. When he waved his hand, my heart sprang up . . ."

They left the gorge for the narrows of a still smaller ravine and there, by a trickle of water, Perique at last lay down.

He stripped the bandage from his arm. It had gripped the flesh with hard fingers. The blood no longer flowed. The skin, purple-gray, puckered at the mouth of the ragged wound, filled to the lips with a black, congealing welter of blood. Konia moaned once and then was silent, holding the arm with fingers as delicate as thought.

"Can you make a needle out of a bit of hard bamboo, Konia?" asked Perique. "And thread out of the finest fibers?"

"Yes, lord," said Konia.

"Make the needle and find the thread. I am going to sleep,

170

Konia."

He closed his eyes. The cool of the ground soaked into his body and drew the fever out. From the bright streak of water that ran beside him, he had drunk once, deeply. Thirst commenced again, but it must not be allowed to have its way. A body weighted with water is like a soggy sponge, good for nothing. Through the lashes of his eyes, he watched the blue of the sky for a moment. The blood was beginning to force its way through the numbed flesh of his right arm; the pain doubled and redoubled.

He took the edge of his will, like a knife, and removed from his nervous system that wounded arm and all its concerns. Then he slept. Afterward Konia was there. The sense of her nearness roused him, brought him slowly up through the deep, dark well of slumber to the brink of daylight consciousness.

"Konia, have you made the needles and found the thread?" he asked.

"Yes, lord," she said, and held up the fine fibers and the little sharp-pointed splits of the bamboo.

"Do you know what they're for?" asked Perique.

"No, lord."

"You're going to wash this wound until the blood runs from it again, and then you'll sew up the lips of it neatly, pulling them close together with the thread and needle."

She said nothing.

"Yes, lord," she whispered.

"Do you understand, Konia?"

She washed the wound. She sat down cross-legged and took the limp weight of the arm across her lap. A bamboo needle tentatively pricked the arm of Perique, jerked back.

"Deeper, Konia. Deeper," he said. "Drive the needle right down and in and pull the thread through briskly, or otherwise we'll never be done. So! So! That's better. I can tell without looking that you're doing it properly, now. If you keep on crying, how can you do the sewing properly? There

171

is nothing to cry about. I have put this sick arm away from my mind. I have nothing to do with it. Press the raw flesh inside, Konia. Don't let it protrude. Make the stitches close together. Konia, will you stop crying?"

"Yes, lord," she said. He watched the steady coursing of the tears, looking up at her.

When he was silent, he saw her struggling silently. He watched the tremor of her lips and the grim set of the teeth behind them. And still she thrust the bamboo needle deeply through the flesh of his arm.

"Now," said Perique, "you have finished, and it's an excellent piece of work. That arm will heal as safely as though the best doctor in the world had worked on it. Konia, will you find me food of some sort?"

"Yes, lord. Is the pain very terrible?"

"Find me something to eat. I have to sleep now, and afterwards I must eat. And by sunset I must be near Tupia again."

"Tupia?" cried Konia, bewildered.

"Yes," said Perique. "Even with only one hand to talk for me, I must go back to Tupia tonight."

CHAPTER 31

There was a party at Matthew Coffee's house, that night. It would hardly have been right for Coffee himself to give such a big affair, considering that he was a bankrupt, but everybody who was anybody in Tupia flooded into the Coffee house bringing along whole hampers of delicacies. For drink, of course, they still could depend upon the deep cellars of Matthew Coffee, and in fact there was a celebration that extended all the way from the famous "cool room" to the gardens of the house. And a whacking big silver moon came up and shone on the party.

Perique, with his wounded arm supported in a sling made of soft, old fishnet, paused in the dark of some palms near the house of Coffee and listened to the celebration for a time.

Konia said, in the black of the shadows: "You see, lord, there are so many of them. And although your heart is greater than ever, you have only one hand, and Konia's two hands are only a small help."

"So go home to your father's house, Konia."

"As if I could leave you, lord, when—"

"Go home to your father's house, Konia."

She found him with her hands in the darkness.

"Will you say farewell to me, lord?"

She whispered the cry of lament. He put his arm around her.

"If you feel me trembling, lord, it is for happiness," she said. "You can feel that my body is clean. For many days I have not put on the coconut oil."

"You ought to, though, Konia. Because the oil is a great comfort against the sun."

"But white people have strange noses and the smell of the oil makes their noses wrinkle. My lips also are clean, lord."

"That white man's habit of kissing is a silly thing," said Perique.

"If you kiss me, lord, no other man shall ever touch me with the tip of a finger in passing."

"That's why I won't kiss you, Konia."

"If my skin were not a dirty yellow, and if there were no smoke in my eyes, could my lord have loved Konia?"

"Shall I tell you something, Konia? A grown man cannot weep, but my heart is aching. If I die tonight, the last thing I shall think of will be Konia."

She was silent for a time. "That is enough," she said at last. "I can remember that—now that we stand apart again, how cold the wind blows me! How many days shall I weep before my eyes are dry again? Farewell, lord."

He heard her go. Afterward he went carefully through

173

shadows, avoiding the moon, until he came to the house of Harrison Lee. It was not a mansion like the spreading courts and buildings of Matthew Coffee. It was merely raised on a terrace of uncemented stones and built in semi-native style, except that there was a long veranda overlooking the sea. The kitchen was a separate little building behind the house, and food was carried into it along a covered walk.

Perique had studied that house so well, before this night, that he knew where he wanted to go. He left his shoes behind him, taking a worn fold of paper from under the inner sole of one of them and putting it away in a trouser pocket. The trip through the canebrake had turned him into a ragged tramp, covered with a thousand scratches and bruises; but the ache of his wounded arm was now only a subdued throbbing to which he could afford to pay no attention.

His bare feet crossed the veranda with a tentative tread that softened before a commencing squeak in the boards could mature to a really audible sound. The door he did not **try, but stole close** to an open window inside of which a light was shining. Over the sill of the low window he had a glimpse of Nancy Lee, who sat facing the sea, with her hands folded in her lap, her eyes closed. She was not sleeping. The pain in her face was too livid and real for that.

Perique slunk down the veranda and tried a window two rooms away. He slid it up with no difficulty, but with that water-clock slowness which prevents the making of noise. Afterward he pulled himself into the dark of the room within. He was about to light a match, but here the trotting of hoofs of a horse stopped outside the house and he heard someone running up the steps.

He went back to the window to watch and saw Lieutenant Clifford of the constabulary hurrying down the veranda.

"Nancy!" called the lieutenant. "Ah, there you are."

"What is it?" asked Nancy Lee, her voice coming small and clear to Perique.

"Why, everyone's at the Coffee place and nothing goes on

well without you, Nancy."

"I've tried to go. I've dressed to go," she answered. "But I can't, Lawrence."

"I know," said Clifford sympathetically. "It's the finding of the things on the beach. I know it brings it all back with a horrible clearness."

"What I've wondered—could he possibly be alive on the island for some hidden reason of his own?" asked the girl.

"You knew your own father; I knew Harrison Lee, too. Was he a man to go skulking, while his daughter was breaking her heart for him? I understand what you hope: that it was *he* who burned his own sea-chest because, mysteriously, he needed to disappear. But what of the knife in the tree? What of his coat that Perique was found wearing?"

She, after a pause, said in a weary voice: "It was Perique, then? You're sure, Lawrence?"

"As sure as I am that Perique is dead."

"But *are* you sure of that?"

"Where could he have gone, Nancy? Only one place. Over the edge of the cliff. A desperate man that wouldn't face justice—much readier to face death. He simply jumped out from the edge of the rock. The body easily could have been shunted from a lower face of the cliff into the river; and by this time it's washing out to sea.

"I'm sorry, Nancy. I know it's sickening. But it's justice, too. I shouldn't ask you now to come over to Coffee's place, but we all feel that we have to make a last effort to send poor Matthew away with a warm welcome. God knows that he's been an honest man, and a brave man when the crash came to him. I never saw a finer thing than the way he met the robbery, and the smashing of his whole life of work."

"I know," said Nancy Lee. "And I'll go, too. I won't let myself be a baby."

"Ah, good girl," said the lieutenant. "I heard Matthew ask after you. When he found you weren't there, I saw him take in a breath and drop his eye, but he only said: 'Of course she isn't here. She couldn't come here. I understand, poor girl!' "

"I'm coming right out," said Nancy Lee.

So, a moment later, Perique watched her go down the steps to where the carriage of Lieutenant Clifford waited for her; and it went jouncing up the rough street toward the house of Matthew Coffee.

Then Perique turned and lighted his match. He was in a small study, the walls of it lined with crowded bookshelves, a big rollertop desk in a corner.

Before the light of that match died, he had closed the shutters of the window through which he entered. Now he ignited a lamp, turned the wick low, and started to work on the desk. It was locked. He took the butt of his revolver and smashed that lock. Then he sat down and smoked a cigarette.

A single noise almost never rouses a house, even the explosion of a gun. There are too many explanations—the falling of a chair—the dropping of something heavy—a stroke of thunder. The single noise makes people lift their heads; it is the second disturbance that makes them go searching for the cause of the trouble.

When his cigarette was finished, Perique resumed his work. The top of the roller desk now lifted, unhindered, and showed him the conventional rows of pigeon-holes stuffed full of papers. These were of no apparent interest to him. He opened the drawers, one by one, giving each hardly more than a glance, until he came to a mass of old charts, stacked together. These he shuffled out on the floor one after the other, scanning the face of each with care.

A dozen he had found before he located something on one of them that held his eye. He put the single chart on top of the desk, unfolded the worn paper still in his pocket, and laid it down beside a place on the printed chart where all the lines had been darkened by pencil strokes.

The comparison lasted only a moment. He refolded his paper, restored it to his pocket, shuffled the charts together, pushed them back into the drawer from which he had taken them. The rest of the confusion in the room he left just as he had made it, and putting out the light, he was quickly through the window, gliding from shadow to shadow with those bare, silent feet.

He went up again toward the house of Matthew Coffee, with the sound of the music to guide even a blind man.

Pain and exhaustion had taken some of the fine bloom from his attention, unstrung his nerves a little, dulled all his senses. For, otherwise, he surely would have been aware of the figure that followed him, moving with equally subtle care from shadow to shadow.

Instead, he slipped close in under the wall of the house and only once paused to turn and stare all about him with those suspicious eyes; that was before he clambered up to a window whose shutters were locked. The lock troubled him only a moment, then the shutters opened, admitted him, and he was closed again into the darkness of a room.

CHAPTER 32

Matthew Coffee was to leave Tupia at once, and his goods were packed for the journey. He could have taken everything in his house to set up a home in Old England, and never a voice in Lanua would have been raised in protest, but the integrity of Matthew Coffee would not permit him to do so. Only the strong persuasion of the governor and of Captain Wilshire could induce him to take even his most personal belongings.

The rest was to be put up at sale to realize what it might in the name of his creditors.

So there stood in the room of Coffee, prepared for the voyage, only a battered little canvas trunk, reinforced at the bottom with a slab of wood, and banded with heavy straps. There was also a flexible, old-fashioned valise. Both were packed except for a slight space at the top of the valise, into which toilet articles could be put.

Perique locked the door, lighted a lamp and a cigarette, and sitting down cross-legged beside the valise went through it to the bottom. The clothes he left strewn about the floor.

The bottom of the valise he worked, and found it flexible. Then he turned with a sigh to the trunk.

He unbuckled the straps of the trunk which, because of the straps, was not locked, and at once was busy with the contents.

He hardly used his eyes. Touch was swifter and more accurate. But every garment he crumpled thoroughly in the grasp of his big hand before he dropped it to the floor.

It made slow work, work so slow that once or twice a sweat started on the face of Perique, and he glanced toward the door. But he would not abate in his thoroughness until every article was out of the trunk, and he was left to stare hopelessly into the empty interior.

He rose, shook his head, and stared gloomily around him at all parts of the room. There was the bed, for instance, that might be searched—but when he had taken a stride toward it, he turned about again, led by a sullen determination, and turned the trunk upside down. The solid slab of board he touched, tapped softly. Then, pulling out his knife, he opened the blade with his teeth and carved into the wood. The edge gritted on something much harder. When he looked at the table, he could see an inch of flattened edge.

And at that his face lighted.

Again he put the trunk right side up but stopped to listen to a throng of footfalls that poured down the hall outside the room. At the door of Coffee's room they paused.

The knob of the door turned, was shaken. Perique already had sprung across the room to the shuttered windows, but as he pushed the shutters wide, he found himself looking down at a squad of half a dozen of the constabulary, all armed to the teeth.

Perique went back into a corner of the room and sat down. He took out his revolver and held it steady across his knee.

Here the voice of Captain Wilshire called out: "Perique! We know you're there and we've got you. Will you surrender peacefully or do you intend to fight like a mad dog?"

Perique called out: "Why not have a little quiet talk, Wilshire? You must have another key to that door. Come in, all of you, and we'll have the talk."

Out in the street voices were shouting; they had seen the apparition at the window, and they seemed to know what it meant. "Perique!" they chanted, like the one word of a long song.

In the hallway there were murmurings, and then the door was unlocked. Wilshire said: "Be careful, Clifford!"

Lieutenant Clifford said: "Somebody has to be the first man in."

And straightway he stepped into the room. Others pushed right in behind him. Matthew Coffee himself, Wilshire, and the tall figure of the Honorable Irvine, with even one woman who managed to slip in with the leaders. That was Nancy Lee.

In the middle of the floor they saw the opened trunk and valise. And in the corner sat Perique with the muzzle of the big revolver pointed casually toward them and a cigarette fuming in his lips. Two days' beard darkened his face. His trousers were in tatters, his body naked to the waist and covered with a thousand small abrasions. A wind seemed to be blowing through his hair.

Matthew Coffee said: "The cur has had to dirty my clothes with his hands! It's almost a pity, Wilshire, that there is no special punishment for a murderer who's *also* a thief."

"I've stolen nothing, Coffee," said Perique.

"You didn't intend to, did you?" asked Coffee, sneering.

Some of the constabulary officers were edging down along the walls of the room. Perique said: "You fellows keep back for a while, will you? In ten minutes I'll surrender to the law without striking a blow but I want those ten minutes to use as I please."

"Take him and knock him on the head," urged Coffee, as he stared at the litter of clothes on the floor.

Lieutenant Clifford remarked: "I think we'll accept that promise, Captain Wilshire?"

"I suppose so," said the captain. "What do you want with ten minutes, Perique? You're not to be lynched. This is not your own precious country. You'll have decent interval in the jail before you're hanged."

"Hanged for what?" asked Perique.

"The murder of Tom Lawson and Ellis, and Jackie the night watchman; and for connivance or the whole blame for the sinking of the ship *Nancy Lee* with the crew on board her."

"That's plenty of murder," agreed Perique. "By the way, I suppose it was your neat little brain, Clifford, that located me in this room?"

Clifford flushed a bit under the stroke, but he shrugged his shoulders.

"One of my men saw the girl Konia," he said. "When he saw her sneaking through the night, he thought of Perique. She should have been mourning at home for the dead man; instead, she was slipping along like a cat through the night. She was following you, Perique. That was what pointed the way for us."

"Ah!" said Nancy Lee.

"Perique, let's get you out of here," said Wilshire. "Just put aside that gun!"

"I have plenty of the ten minutes left," said Perique. "You fellows speak of hanging the man who murdered the good ship *Nancy Lee* and the crew on board her. Do you know what should be done with him? He ought to be staked out where the ants could eat him. Suppose I tell you what the last minute was like on that ship. There was the wind smashing the waves white on the reef; and the ship driving

180

straight on to her finish; and poor Harry Lee standing alone on that deck, until I joined him."

"Harry Lee alone?" cried Nancy. "Where was the crew?"

"Dead—or asleep—snoring like cattle, scattered over the deck. A lot of good sailors among those Lanuans; but they might have been too lively in the water. They might have escaped the teeth of the reef, so they were drugged in the round of rum they'd had just as the ship sighted the light— the light that should have been on Nihoni Point. There wasn't a man of the lot fit for anything.

"When I heard Harry Lee shouting, I ran up from my place in the hold where I'd been stowed away since Kandava. And there I found Lee like a man and a hero. And dead swine lay useless on the decks all around him. I tried to give a hand; but then we struck. He had time to throw his sea-chest into the sea. But the reef got him with its shark's teeth. I was the one that rode the chest ashore."

"Why don't you keep your curious story for the magistrate?" asked Captain Wilshire with contempt.

"Because the story comes to an end here in this room," said Perique. "Before Lee died, he had a chance to tell me that it was murder, not rum, that killed the *Nancy Lee* and the men on board her."

"Who would have doped the rum?" demanded Lieutenant Clifford.

"The fellow who left the ship before she reached the narrows and swam ashore with the cream of the pearl cargo? Captain Ellis, of course," said Perique. "You worked out that part of the problem yourself, Clifford."

The Honorable Irvine said: "You know, my dear fellows, I don't see the reasons for the whole thing."

"The reason's here," said Perique.

Without putting the revolver from his hand, he pulled out the old fold of paper and threw it out on the floor.

"There's a bit of a chart of a corner of the Solomon Islands that Harrison Lee copied from an Admiralty chart.

Take a look at it."

Captain Wilshire, scowling, unfolded the paper.

"The ten minutes of the rascal are about up," said Matthew Coffee. "If you'll give me a chance to clear up my room again, Wilshire . . ."

Captain Wilshire, not even hearing, was saying: "What is one to see in this chart?"

"Pearls, captain," said Perique. "You see the two crosses? The end of a pearl bed rich enough to put a wind in the King of England's sails. Harrison Lee found it on the voyage before the last. The crew of his Lanuans and Ellis, the captain, went crazy about the richness of that pearl bed. You may remember that when they made harbor after the last voyage, the crew hardly went ashore. Provisions were thrown on board. There was a hasty conference between the commanders and Matthew Coffee. And then the *Nancy Lee* sailed again. That crew had been bribed to the gills to keep it from talking about the great new pearl fishery that had been uncovered. Does this make sense?"

Lieutenant Clifford said, through his teeth: "It begins to make the best sense in the world. Just a minute, Captain Wilshire. Let's hear this out."

Nancy Lee, sitting in a chair in a corner of the room, stared across at Perique with fascinated eyes.

"They got away to the second voyage," said Perique, "but not until they'd made the arrangement—Ellis and one man on shore—for the stealing of the pearls and the smashing of the *Nancy Lee,* and the murder of every other man in the world who knew about the new fishery. That fishery was to be exploited by people who would keep the profits.

"A complicated scheme it sounds, but not when you think of people willing to do that simple little murder of poor Tom Washburn. With him out of the way, the Nihoni Point light could burn at another place, for one night. Somebody with a strong glass, watching carefully, would see the rig of the *Nancy Lee* while she was still far out to sea, far out in

182

the afternoon light.

"Take her several hours to run into the harbor and that left time to kill Washburn and change the light."

Clifford said: "This is the truth, and nothing but the truth. It has the right ring. Perique, I suppose you'll hang for it, but if you pose as an honest man, can you give us a ghost of an explanation of the things you've been doing on this island and the part you've been playing?"

"Suppose for a moment," said Perique, "that I'm telling the truth when I say that I was on board the *Nancy Lee* when she struck. Suppose that I saw one of the finest men in God's world being sent to his death surrounded by a pack of poor, drugged Islanders; suppose that I knew it was murder and decided that I'd run down the dirty killers?"

"I'll try to suppose," said the lieutenant. "But . . . Perique, there'll never be any proof to help your story unless we could find the pearls themselves."

"Why not?" said Perique. "They're in the room here with you. They're where the murder-in-chief put them, the fellow who counted for Jackie, too, and then murdered his confederate, Ellis, with that little device of the safe. They're in the false bottom of that trunk, if it's worth your while to open it and look. Five minutes more and I would have found them myself!"

CHAPTER 33

They looked at Matthew Coffee with the open eyes of horrified children. He started to say: "Don't try to—don't—"

Then the weight of those horrified glances smashed him. He muttered, "Oh, my God!" and pulled a gun from under his coat.

He had no chance to use it on himself. Every man in the room had jumped for him.

He was crushed back against the wall under a pressure of many hands. The gun was torn away from him.

The Honorable Irvine, governor of Lanua, rubbed his red nose tenderly and said: "What? Really? Honest Matt Coffee a murderer? . . . Well, well, well! There are things in this world as strange as Perique! Absolutely as strange, upon my word of honor."

They kept Coffee pinned. His head fell on his breast like a dying man, nerveless, inert.

And the bottom of the trunk, in the meantime, was smashed to pieces.

The pearls were there. Six small chamois skin sacks of them, and one soft little package all by itself. The lootings of a rich fishery indeed. Three or four hundred thousand dollars' worth of gems, and among them one huge beauty that seemed to half fill the hollow of a palm, pure, flawless as the full moon, an enchanting loveliness.

It brought a muttering and then a silence through the room.

Then the voice of Wilshire called out: "Where's Perique! You blind fools, have you let Perique get away? After him. He's sick with his wound. He can't get far . . ."

"Just a moment, everyone," said the Honorable Irvine, lifting a hand that stopped the stampede at once.

He cleared his throat and looked about him with his drink-bleared eyes.

"My dear lads," said the governor, "it's true that there's still a price on the head of Perique; but I don't think that that money would be worth anything to the honest people on the island of Lanua. Does everyone follow me in this? Do you all follow me in this, gentlemen?"

And, for the first time in many years, the governor was in fact followed.

Captain Wilshire merely said: "Considering everything—yes, you're right!"

And so said the whole island of Lanua. The head-money

of Perique, the blood money for that wanderer, would not have been worth a penny in the pocket of any man on the island.

They turned back from the thought of Perique to the soggy vision of that broken man, Matthew Coffee.

Nancy Lee, going home to the loneliness of her house, kept looking from the dark of the ground to the brightness of the stars.

And sometimes there were tears in her eyes, and sometimes she was smiling.

Perhaps not once during that walk did she care to remember that her own little fortune was restored, now that the loot of Matthew Coffee became the property of the subscribers to his company.

But when she came to the veranda of her house, she bade Lieutenant Clifford good-by.

And when he had gone off into the night, she sat alone on the veranda.

"Well, Nancy?" said a voice at the end of the veranda.

"Is it you, Perique?" she asked.

"I stopped around to say good-by," said Perique. "Don't turn your head. I'm not good to see."

"I'm going to take you inside; I'm going to take care of you!" said Nancy Lee, and started up from her chair.

A hand irresistibly strong held her shoulder and pressed her back into her chair again.

"You'd even dress me up in his clothes, Nancy," said Perique. "But it won't do. Listen to me. When I saw you the first time, I knew his blood was in you. He was as fine a man as I ever saw, as brave and as steady in the pinch. After I saw you, I began to see you even when my eyes were closed."

"And I helped them to hunt you down!" said the girl. "I—"

"That was part of the game."

"Perique, let me—"

"Steady," said Perique. "We could be a pair of sentimental fools in no time, couldn't we? Beautiful, good girl—big strong man with a fine big cut on his arm—all that sort of thing. But you know what I am, Nancy. We can't let ourselves go, can we?"

"No," said the girl.

He drew unseen and unheard, a slow, deep breath. Then she said: "You'll go where?"

"There's always plenty of wind blowing around the South Seas," he said.

"Will it blow you back to Lanua?"

"How could it help, someday?" he asked. "Good-by, Nancy."

"I—Perique!"

"Look here," said Perique. "I seem something valuable, just now. But I'm not.

"Or whatever I am, it's better for us to have a few days of open water between us. Is that right?"

She covered her face with her hands.

"Is that right?" he insisted.

"Yes," she said.

"Shall I go now?"

"Yes," said the girl.

Afterward, she waited, incredulous. Then, hopeful when she heard no sound, "Perique!" she murmured.

There was no answer. She jumped to her feet.

"Perique!" she cried, but the cry was only a whisper.

The veranda was empty. Nothing moved between her and the stars.

When the shadow stepped over the threshold of the house of Kohala, Liho sprang to his feet, and Kohala himself sat entranced with astonishment.

But Perique murmured to them: "It's safe. They are hunting me no longer."

186

He could speak like that unheard by Konia.

She sat cross-legged, her arms crossed before her face while she swayed a little from side to side and uttered the old lament which was timeless among her people and which runs like this:

> You have left us; you have risen from us;
> We sink into darkness as into water;
> But the way that you travel far above us
> Is among a thousand, thousand lights.

Kohala motioned to Liho and led him out of the hut into the open night, past the tall, battered figure of Perique.

"What will happen?" asked Liho.

"Who can tell?" asked Kohala.

"Has he only come to say good-by?" asked the boy.

"My heart is too old to understand or know," said Kohala.

"She stops singing," whispered Liho. "She cries out; she sees him!"

"Hush!" said Kohala.

"There is nothing to hear. There is only silence," said Liho. "Why are they silent?"

"Ah," said Kohala, "that I am still young enough to know."